Cedarwood Pride

STARTING OVER IN CEDARWOOD

MEGAN SLAYER

Starting Over in Cedarwood
ISBN # 978-1-83943-721-2
©Copyright Megan Slayer 2021
Cover Art by Erin Dameron-Hill ©Copyright July 2021
Interior text design by Claire Siemaszkiewicz
Pride Publishing

Published in 2021 by Pride Publishing, United Kingdom.

Pride Publishing is an imprint of Totally Entwined Group Limited.

Collections
What's his Passion?: Wild Card
Love's Bloom: Love Next Door
Sun, Sea and…: Sun, Sea and Summer Songs

STARTING OVER
IN CEDARWOOD

Dedication

For the Lucky Ducks, JPZ and TPZ

Chapter One

"What a great day to visit the ballfield," Shaun Fallows said. He breathed in the fresh air and scent of freshly cut grass. "The weather's perfect, there's a slight breeze and just the right amount of clouds and sun."

Warrick rolled his eyes. "You're too invested in this already. We're just here for the newspaper. If old Mr. Nicholas weren't so busy playing house, he'd be here, too."

Shaun shrugged to hide his excitement. He'd been to ballfields before and had even covered a couple of games for his high school paper as well as his hometown paper, but those had been small fields and tiny teams. This was the Cedarwood Wildcats. This was the bigger time. Besides, he didn't give a shit if Mr. Nicholas, the head of the paper, was home with his husband. *More power to them.*

"Sucks. Mr. N should be here and directing this, not us." Warrick pointed to the luxury boxes. "We're up there."

Shaun whipped his card out and showed the attendant, then strode through the gate to the executive level. The ballfield wasn't that big, but he didn't care. He'd arrived. "We're supposed to be enjoying ourselves." He drank in the view. The manicured field stretched out before him and the seats were filled with fans. Flags waved out beyond centerfield and the scent of bread lingered in the air. "We must be near the bakery."

"The bun warmer," Warrick grumbled. "If Mr. N wanted to treat us, then he could've given us a bonus, not made it newspaper day at the ballfield."

"You'll complain about anything, won't you?" Shaun wandered up to the glass windows facing the field. "This is fantastic." He shoved his hands into his pockets and listened to the noise from the crowd as well as the pregame announcements. Once he heard the jingle for the newspaper, his heart swelled.

Ever since he'd nabbed the advertising head position with the paper, his life had seemed to turn around. He had a stable job, a decent apartment and his man trouble wasn't so bad—granted, he didn't have a man, but so what? He'd worry about dating later.

"Everyone." Remy Nicholas, the infamous Mr. N, clapped his hands. "Everyone."

Shaun turned his attention to his boss. Unlike Warrick, Shaun liked Remy. He appreciated Remy's unconventional approach to the paper, printing and having the main version online. Remy had instituted audio versions and pdf versions sent to the schools. He'd even created a video channel for special content.

Remy clapped his hands again. "I know this wasn't the newspaper appreciation day you were all looking forward to, but I wanted to do something different.

This year, we've managed to improve circulation and add jobs. Hits on the website are up and the feedback we're getting is off the charts. Thank you to those who helped with the school supply collection. That went so well. The kids of Cedarwood will appreciate your hard work. For those who are assisting this Tuesday with the food drive, know your help will make the difference. People are paying attention to the social media posts and the little live events, so keep it up."

Shaun applauded. He hadn't been able to donate time to the school supply drive, but he'd signed up to help with the food one.

"Now, the reason for having the newspaper appreciation day here at the field was to give back. I want you to have a nice day at the ballpark, but also to get us into the community. Enjoy yourselves. The bar is open and food is ready. Thank you for being the best staff and for continued great times with the newspaper," Remy said. "Thank you."

"God, he gets long-winded," Warrick said. He applauded, but sighed. "I hate baseball."

"I don't care." Shaun wasn't a fan of negative people. He'd had enough of that in his relationship with Jonah. No matter what he'd done, Jonah hadn't been happy. Never the right clothes, the right shoes...his hair wasn't cut properly or was too long...and the arguments. He didn't miss the arguments.

Two men in black shirts and trousers wheeled a cart into the room. One man took his position behind the hot dog stand and the other wheeled the empty cart out. The man pushing the cart caught Shaun's attention. He had a thing for tall, dark and handsome men. The way the guy's brown hair flopped over his brow and his eyes glittered sent a shiver along Shaun's spine. The man turned and, when he smiled, the dimple in his cheek became more prominent and Shaun noticed the beauty mark along his jawline. Warmth enveloped Shaun. He hadn't had a reaction like this in so long.

"Who is that?" Shaun murmured. "The guy with the cart."

"That?" Warrick chuckled. "That's Kevin Keiser. He runs the food service center here at the ballfield. Quiet guy. I think he's single and I'm fairly sure he's gay." He elbowed Shaun. "Are you gay? I never asked."

"It wasn't your business, but yes, I am." Shaun swept his gaze over Kevin again. Kevin looked trim in his food service outfit, but strong, too.

Cara, one of the girls from the accounting department of the paper, sidled up to Shaun. "Are you eyeballing Kevin?"

"Maybe." He bowed his head to stop gawking. "Is that bad?"

"Other than you look like you want to eat him, you're staring so hard?" She laughed. "No, it's not bad. He's a nice guy."

"I hear he's quiet." Shaun managed to get through the food line, but didn't see Kevin again. Instead of sitting with Warrick, he ended up at the table with Cara. "Do you know Kevin?"

"Went to school with him." She nodded and settled next to Shaun. "He doesn't talk much. Never did. I think it's because he got teased so mercilessly in school. Everyone but him knew he was gay and teased him, then it got worse once he came out. It was bad, but he seemed to keep his head up, especially once he admitted he was gay."

"I see." Shaun watched the baseball game, but stole glances over at the service stations in case Kevin came back. Shaun nudged Cara. "Do you think he'd give me the time of day if I asked him for his number?"

"You?" She coughed, then sipped her water. "Honey, you're sexy. If he doesn't, it's because he's scared." Once she cleared her throat and finished her water, she nodded. "I mean, he's shy, so he might not say 'yes, I want your number', but he'd be crazy if he turned you down. You're handsome."

"Handsome doesn't mean much sometimes." Shaun finished his hot dog and toyed with his fries. He managed to smear ketchup on his fingers. "Do you have a napkin?"

"Nope. I forgot to grab one." Cara groaned. "And I need one. Please?"

"Sure." He left the table and headed toward the service station. "Hi, I could use some napkins."

The teenager offered up a stack. "Sorry. They stick together and don't clean up much unless you have five."

"Thanks." He accepted the bundle, then glanced over his shoulder. Kevin still hadn't come back. Maybe he'd been an apparition. Shaun settled at the table with Cara and divided the napkins. "Good?"

"Very. Thank you." She blotted her mouth, then groaned again. "Not today."

"What?" Shaun balled his paper, then glanced about the room. "What's wrong?"

"Warrick's being a pain in the ass." She massaged her forehead. "He's complaining about the food."

"There's nothing wrong with it," Shaun said. "Standard ballfield food, but it's not bad." That said, his coworker wasn't a happy man and could find something wrong with a perfect twenty-four-carat gold ring.

"Excuse me. Do you have soggy buns, too?"

Shaun froze, then looked at Cara, who'd gone pale. She hadn't been the one to ask the question and the speaker didn't sound like Warrick. Shaun turned his attention to the one who had spoken. *Kevin.* Shaun's breath lodged in his throat. The man was even more handsome up close. Shaun noted the sprinkling of hairs on Kevin's cheeks and the lines crinkling at the corners of his eyes. Were those flecks of silver at his temples, too?

Kevin cleared his throat. "I'm sorry. The other table is complaining about the buns being subpar. Are your dining choices up to your standards?"

"Uh…" Shaun had to sound intelligent, not silly, but he couldn't manage to form a normal sentence.

"They're great," Cara said. "Thank you."

"Are you sure? We're here to provide a fine dining experience," Kevin said. "At decent prices."

"You sound like you're a walking advertisement," Shaun managed. He balled his hand on his thigh under the table and drew in a deep breath to center himself. He'd never had problems talking to guys before now. "I don't think our buns are soggy." He smiled and met Kevin's gaze. "But I would like to ask you a question." *Christ. Confidence, don't fail me now.*

"Do you need more ketchup? Some of the bottles are low." Kevin shook his head, then reached across the table to retrieve the bottle. "I let Buzz handle it and he only filled about half of them."

"No." Shaun touched Kevin's forearm, stopping him. The move also sent tingles along Shaun's nerve endings. His synapses stood at full alert. "I... Would you like to grab a beer sometime?"

"Oh." Kevin froze and confusion clouded his eyes. "You want to go out with me?"

"I do." Shaun mustered his confidence. "I know it's a strange time to ask you that, but I wasn't sure if I'd get to see you again. It's just beers or coffee, but I'd like to go out sometime with you." *Christ.* He'd managed to stumble over everything he'd just said.

"Uh, sure." Kevin stood at his full height and clasped his hands together. "But you're sure you're happy with the food?"

"Very." Shaun scrawled his number on a piece of paper. "Call me when you're free. I'd like to buy you that beer or coffee."

Kevin tipped his head and a slight smile curled on his lips. A crooked smile. "I will."

When Kevin walked away, Shaun considered what he'd done. "I asked him out."

"You did." Cara elbowed him. "Good for you."

"I asked him out," Shaun repeated. He hadn't wrapped his mind around what he'd done. *Holy shit.*

"It's the crooked smile, isn't it? He is adorable." She collected the trash on the table. "He got that smile when he was a kid. Auto accident, I think. It messed up his jaw and he's got a scar. I think he had surgery to have the damage made less visible." She stood. "I'm going to toss this then sit along the window. Care to join me?"

"Sure." He picked up his beer and followed her over to the window. The game was already in full swing. "Who's winning?"

"We are, by two." She settled on one of the chairs. "If I wasn't neck-deep in kids and getting mine through junior high, I'd toss my hat into the dating game, but I have no time."

"Give it a shot." He sat beside her. "So you went to school with Kevin? Has he been single long?"

"A year, I think."

"That's a shame. He's cute." No, he was fucking hot—not that he'd tell Cara as much. Most of the cute guys he knew were already married or in long-term relationships.

"The shame is that he's too picky." Cara laughed. "Not that I can complain. I'm forty-one and not remarried or even dating."

"You don't look your age." So Kevin was roughly forty-one, too? Only a year or so younger than him. *Good.* "What do you mean, he's picky? Being selective is good."

"He doesn't date anyone who isn't approved by his cat," she said. "You hate cats, so you'd better just have one beer with him and cut your losses, now that I think about it."

"I don't hate cats." He hadn't found one that liked him, but that was beside the point. "Are he and the cat that close?"

"Very."

Shaun shrugged. Cara was probably exaggerating. She tended to when she discussed something dramatic. The car accident was always the worst she'd ever seen or her kid scoring a goal was always the best goal ever in the history of eighth grade hockey. "I'll give him a chance."

"Who?" Warrick found them and sat beside Shaun. "Dave? Don't date Dave. He's full of himself. Plus, you'll smell like you've bathed in his cologne."

Shaun shrugged again. Their co-worker, Dave, did tend to wear his aftershave a bit on the thick side. Everyone who hugged him tended to smell like him.

"Shut up," Dave said. "I heard our Shaun gave Kevin Keiser his digits."

"Keiser? He's so quiet," Warrick said. "He's gay? Oh wait. I knew that. He had a guy…Kyle someone or another. I guess they had a falling out."

"Over the cat," Cara said.

Shaun gritted his teeth to keep from speaking. Kevin's personal life wasn't their business. "You need to leave him alone."

"Why? He had a fight with a guy over a cat. The critter hated Kyle, I think," Warrick said. He shrugged, then downed some of his beer. "If I can't find a woman to get along with Patrice, then it's a nonstarter."

"Your dog?" Dave snorted. "It's just a dog."

"Might be to you, but she's a good dog," Warrick said. "She's more loyal than you've ever been."

Shaun snorted. "You two." He ignored the rest of the conversation in favor of the baseball game. "Kevin seemed nice and I went out on a limb. It might not work, but I won't know unless we go out, so there."

"You should give him a shot," Cara said. "You'd be good for him. You're quiet and smart like him. Maybe you'd bring each other out of your shell."

"Maybe." His thoughts turned to Kevin. He hadn't felt sparks like that in ages and he liked the rush. He missed the delight of being with someone and being wanted. Hell, he liked being part of a relationship.

Besides, he was tired of the one-night stands and pretty boys who only wanted him to pump up their ego or be their sugar daddy. He was only forty-two, but sometimes he felt ancient. He worked hard for his money and the paper. Could Kevin be the one he'd been looking for?

He hoped so.

* * * *

Kevin pushed the cart of soggy buns to the food prep station in the bowels of the stadium. The silly mistakes, like overheating and allowing the buns to get soggy, wore him out. Why couldn't the workers do their jobs? No one seemed to listen to him and he'd worked too hard to make the concessions decent dining. Granted, hot dogs and chili dogs weren't high cuisine, but he refused to sell soggy buns.

"What happened?" Kevin tossed the rack of buns into the food bin. "I can't sell these. Can't give them away, either." He closed the bin door. "We're measured by the quality of the food, and this isn't quality."

Gus shrugged. "I messed up and listened to Buzz. He said to set the warming rack too high and the condensation got to those buns. I thought they'd dry out, but they didn't."

"No, they didn't." Kevin hated being on the floor. He hated having to interact with the customers, too. His forte was numbers and stats. How to make the food better and how to get the bigger bang for the buck, that was his thing. He tended to get too emotional when the product wasn't right. Right now, the buns being soggy weren't his issue. Mistakes happened and he understood that. What aggravated him was wasting food and the sloppy mistakes. He'd told Gus a hundred times not to set the warmer too high and the tray of ruined buns equaled a sloppy mistake.

Nedra shook her head. "That's what we get for letting Buzz help. It's on me and I'm sorry. I thought he'd learned, but no."

"Put him back on dishes and cleaning." Kevin tossed the second tray of buns. "I had to explain to the people from the paper that we made a mistake. It was embarrassing."

"I'm sure." She wiped the trays down. "To make matters worse, you're going to have to help with the after-game banquet. Nathen Clarke quit and we don't have anyone to do the beer chest."

"Of course." *Fuck.* "Okay."

"He said he got a better offer." She shrugged. "He gave no notice other than leaving."

Kevin sighed to center himself. Getting angry would only increase his blood pressure. "Let's start setting up for the banquet. It's already the ninth inning and we don't have much time."

He left the cart in the kitchen and hurried to the banquet room. The space only sat about fifty people, and according to the schedule, only twenty-five would be attending this gathering. The newspaper wanted to have a nice dinner after the game to congratulate the workers and he was expected to feed them.

The buffet was already set up by the time he arrived and only the beer chest needed attention. He sighed. *Perfect.* He could open beers for the next two hours. Tonya would be in soon and she'd take over as floor manager, so if someone had a complaint, they could go to her.

The people filtered into the room and Kevin pasted on his best, but fake, smile. He didn't like working the buffets and today wasn't a good day. He opened the bottles of beer and handed them to each attendant.

When he swept his gaze across the room, he spotted the guy from the loge. *Damn.* He'd forgotten to ask his name and hadn't bothered to look at his number on the paper. Maybe they'd get a chance to chat again. This time, he'd exchange names.

Nedra elbowed him. "Your ex is here."

Just as she'd spoken the words, Kevin noticed his ex-boyfriend sitting with his mystery man. *Well, hell.* Kyle could be charming and sweet. He was also better looking than Kevin, even on Kevin's best day. If the mystery guy wanted Kyle, then that was his prerogative.

He kept himself in check as Kyle and the mystery man made their way through the line. If he remembered right, the guy liked light beer. He held on to the edge of the beer chest and waited for the next orders.

"Well, well." Kyle offered a sly grin. "I thought you'd be here. Looks like you've been kicked back to the serving line."

"I'm helping out," Kevin said. "Which type of beer would you like, sir?"

"Sir?" Kyle laughed. "I forgot. You're supposed to be all business-like here in line." He threaded his arm around the mystery man's arm. "This is my new boo, Shaun. Shaun, this is my…this is Kevin."

"We've met," Shaun said. "Hi, Kevin."

"Hi." Kevin gestured to the beers. "What can I get you?"

"A light, please?" Shaun asked. "Thank you."

He offered up the selection and smiled. "Welcome."

Kyle waggled his finger in the direction of the table. "I'll meet you over there."

"You're holding up the line," Kevin said. "Make your choice and you can talk later."

"Oh, I will." Kyle plucked a dark brew from the chest. "Open this."

"Of course." Kevin did, then handed the bottle to Kyle. "Don't stick your hands in the chest again."

"Or you'll have me removed?" Kyle snorted. "Stop." He inched around the chest and stood next to Kevin. "Shaun and I are going out after this. Dancing and clubbing. You know, we're really hitting it off." He dug his elbow into Kevin's ribs. "I'll let you know how the date goes."

Kevin tamped down his frustration. He had no business expressing his feelings at work. "Very well."

"See, that's what bothered me about you," Kyle said. "You don't show your emotions. You're ice cold. This is why no one will ever love you. You're emotionless."

Kevin pressed his lips together to keep from saying something. If Kyle wanted to be petty, then that was his problem.

Kevin refilled the beer chest twice and the time seemed to fly by. When he glanced down at his watch, he realized two hours had passed.

Nedra closed down the salad portion of the buffet and joined him at the beer chest. "Why don't you take a break? You need it. I'll handle this."

"Thanks." Kevin wiped his hands on the towel, then made his way over to the doors leading to the foyer.

"Hey." Shaun jogged up to him. "You look beat. Everything okay?"

"Yeah. I'm fine. I've had my hands in the ice for the last two hours and they're a little cold, but I'll live. Did you enjoy the buffet?" Kevin asked. "Is everything up to standards?" He hated slipping into his business-tone, but the job mattered most.

"It was great. To be honest, I'm stuffed and I'll have to run an extra couple of miles tomorrow to work it off." Shaun hooked his thumbs in his pockets. "Do you run?"

"I do. It helps me manage my stress." He wasn't sure why he'd confessed that, but if Shaun was really a runner, he'd understand.

"I hear you. I'll bet this is a real headache, keeping the food service running smoothly." Shaun grinned. "I'm sorry I didn't tell you my name earlier. I saw you and lost my head."

"Do you want your number back?" He wasn't sure where he'd put the piece of paper. "If you've changed your mind, it's cool."

"Why would I do that?" Shaun frowned. "I asked you out for a drink and I want to go." His frown deepened. "I don't ask if I'm not interested."

"You didn't know my name."

"I said I acted on impulse, but I know it now." Shaun's smile returned. "Would you consider the date?" He pulled a small pad of paper from his back pocket. "What's your number? I'll call you."

"Uh…" Why was he hesitating? Because he'd seen Shaun with Kyle. "It's 555-8731."

"Perfect." Shaun grinned and his eyes sparkled. "I'll text you."

"Sure." Up close, Kevin noticed the flecks of dark blue and green in Shaun's blue eyes. Freckles dotted Shaun's nose and the corner of his mouth quirked each time he smiled. Part of Kevin wanted to dart away and hide. He wasn't good at dating and could be awkward without trying. But part of him wanted to linger with

Shaun a bit more. Electricity crackled between them and he forgot a little of his self-consciousness.

Shaun adjusted the collar of Kevin's shirt. "So, since I bungled this earlier… Hi. I'm Shaun Fallows. It's nice to meet you."

"Shaun, my name is Kevin Keiser and it's my pleasure to meet you, too." He wanted to touch Shaun's hand, but the sound of voices jarred him from his mild Shaun-induced fog. "I should get going. I have to help clean up. One of the servers didn't show and, being the supervisor, I have to jump in," he said. "I hope you do text me, because I don't remember where I put your number."

"Then I will." Shaun shook hands with him. "I like a man who knows how to take charge and how to help out. It's good to have a partner."

"Yeah." He couldn't agree more.

Shaun let go and ducked back into the banquet space. Kevin headed through the kitchen and the safety of the prep area. Talking to Shaun was easier than he'd thought.

"I saw you with that guy. Saw you up on the loge, too. He's cute." Nedra pushed the empty beer chest into the kitchen. "Did he ask you out?"

"He did." Kevin managed to nod. "I think he's interested in Kyle, too."

"I saw he showed up. He's working for the paper? Or is he still doing promotions for the team?" she asked.

"Still with the team." Kevin massaged his temples. "Is the party over?"

"Almost everyone is gone. Mr. Nichols talked to the servers and thanked them. I think once he leaves, the rest will, too." Nedra dumped the ice from the chest.

"Thanks for helping us. We needed you on the buffet line."

"Welcome." He wanted to see Shaun one more time, but he'd have to worry about Shaun later. Right now, he had a job to do and dating wasn't important.

Chapter Two

Shaun waited two days before he texted Kevin. His hands shook as he typed out the message. Part of him wished Kevin would text back, but for all he knew, Kevin was at work and couldn't reply. He tossed his phone onto his desk and rolled backward to put his feet on his open drawer.

Cara stopped in the doorway. "Stuck?"

"Sort of." He'd waited two days to contact Kevin. In some circles, that was plenty of time. In others, it was an eternity, and he'd been out of the dating pool for so long that he feared he'd screwed up.

"Did you call Kevin?" she asked.

"Texted him."

"No answer?"

"Not yet." He'd only just sent the text, and if Kevin wasn't sitting on his phone, he might not reply right away.

"He is shy."

"I know."

She stepped into his office and closed the door. "He also saw you with Kyle."

"Mr. Beglin?" He laced his fingers together. The only Kyle he knew was Kyle Beglin. Was that the infamous ex-boyfriend, Kyle?

"That's his ex."

"Oh shit." He'd stepped in it up to his eyeballs. Kyle was charming enough and chatty, but he wasn't exactly Shaun's type. He wasn't into drinkers, not in the same league as Kyle. The guy must've put back half a dozen beers in the space of two hours. Plus, Kyle bragged too much.

"Yeah, so it might have made Kevin a bit quieter than normal."

"Okay, then what's the story as you know it?" He planted one foot on the floor and nudged the drawer shut with the other, then propped his foot on his bent knee. "Lay it out for me."

"You'll have to ask him and you might have your chance soon—you need to go to the ballfield about advertising and their strategy," she said. "I know they want to discuss dollar dog nights and half-price beers."

"I can do that." He wished he'd been given the heads-up earlier, but whatever. "Right now?"

"I'm delivering the message that you need to be there in half an hour." She offered up a piece of paper. "I don't know why they called the main line, but they did."

"Then I'm on it." He folded the paper up and tucked it into the front pocket of his tablet folio. "I'll be back soon-ish."

"See you."

Shaun headed out to his car and checked to ensure he had everything before he left the offices. *Wallet, keys, phone, tablet, paper and pen.* He zipped his messenger bag shut, then backed out of his parking spot. He drove the twenty minutes across town to the ballfield and parked in the visitor area. Unlike the main areas of the ballpark, the offices were no different from any offices he might find in a bigger city. Bland colors, blocky spaces and no personality.

He checked in with the receptionist, then went to the meeting with the heads of advertising. Kyle sat across from him at the long table. He winked a few times and smiled. Shaun ignored Kyle's advances. This wasn't the time to make eyes at someone. Besides, he'd have to let Kyle down gently that he wasn't interested.

At the end of the meeting, when the rest of the participants — save for Kyle, Shaun and Mr. Armstrong, the owner of the team — left, Kevin ventured into the room.

"Oh." Kevin blushed. "I thought I was early. The memo said four. I'm sorry, Mr. Armstrong."

"You were given the wrong memo." Mr. Armstrong clapped Kevin on the shoulder. "I knew what you were going to mention — the dollar dog nights and half-price beers. I also suggested we do a nacho night. Maybe we can develop a food for each night and have a week-long theme? We'll talk tomorrow." Without another word, Mr. Armstrong left the room.

Kevin paled. "Sure." He locked gazes with Shaun. "Oh."

Kyle rounded the table. "Makes a better impression when you're on time." He winked at Shaun. "I'll see you out to the parking lot."

"Just a moment." Shaun nudged Kyle out of the room and closed the door, giving him some privacy with Kevin. "Are you okay? You look unnerved."

"I'm good." Kevin shook his head. "I'm sorry. I got blindsided by the memo. I know it said four."

"Don't worry about it. Sounded like Mr. Armstrong has some big ideas for you." Shaun reached for Kevin, then second-guessed himself. Maybe Kevin didn't want him getting grabby. "I texted you."

"I just saw it." Kevin blushed. "I have to admit I'm not good at dating or getting close to people. I say the wrong thing and stumble over myself."

"That's okay." Shaun understood Kevin better. "Are you free tonight? Say, seven p.m.?"

"I am." Kevin's blush deepened. "You really want to go out with me?"

"Sure. I hear the Coffee Bar is really good. I'm doing advertising for them through the paper and Joe's a decent guy. We can go there and have drinks." Shaun fixed the wrinkle in Kevin's shirt. He couldn't help himself, but he needed to touch Kevin. Plus, the tingles shooting down his arm spurred him on. He noticed the deep brown ring around the edge of Kevin's irises and his thick lashes. He wanted to kiss this man and taste him. "What do you say?"

Kevin hesitated. "Joe *is* a nice guy, and the Coffee Bar is popular."

"So is that a yes? You'll come with me?"

Kevin toyed with the box of straws. "Okay."

"Okay?" He inched up to Kevin. "You know, awkward isn't bad. It's a sign you're human." He traced his fingertip along the top of Kevin's hand. "You're also handsome, and any man would be lucky to go out with you."

"Yeah?" Kevin's eyes widened.

"Yes." Shaun winked. "I'll see you there at seven. My treat." Before Kevin could argue or change his mind, Shaun grinned then walked away.

Something about Kevin got under Shaun's skin. There was an aching there, like he'd been hurt in his past. Kevin was too sweet a guy to be alone, but if Kyle, one of the pushiest men he'd ever met, had dumped Kevin in a raw way...then it explained a lot. Kyle had probably steamrolled over Kevin trying to get what he wanted. If anything, Kyle embodied bluntness.

Shaun left the ballpark and drove back to the newspaper offices. Along the way, he listened to Mozart. The wordless music grounded him and helped him relax. The tension between his shoulders dissipated and he flexed his fingers on the steering wheel. After a little piano concerto, life wasn't so difficult. He parked, then headed inside. Cara waved to him.

"Hi." He stopped at her desk. "Problem?"

"You have a gentleman outside your office who wants to discuss promotion options for his restaurant, and you need to call Stone McCartney at the animal shelter. They want to place an ad, but also want to do a guest spot in the paper. Feature a shelter pet each week and try to get a few more adopted. It'd be good promotion for everyone."

"Agreed." He took the piece of paper from her, then nodded. "Thanks. Now, who is the guy? I don't want to go in cold and screw up his name."

"Oh, it's Jack Walters-Lord. He runs Jack's Hot Dog Shop. He just wants to advertise that he's open and doing to-go orders." Cara grinned. "I love eating there, but I wish it weren't so bad for my waist."

"Your waist is fine." He folded the paper and tucked it into his pocket. "I'll have to try his food. Thanks." He wandered down to his office and found a man sitting on one of the chairs in the corridor. "Hi." Shaun stuck out his hand. "You must be Jack Walters-Lord."

"I am." Jack stood and shook hands with him. "Thanks for meeting with me."

"Not a problem," Shaun said. "I'm Shaun Fallows, advertising director here at the paper. I'm told you'd like to discuss advertising for your restaurant. Pardon my appearance. I'm rumpled because I was just at the ballfield."

"That's what I'm here for—the advertising, not the rumpled part." Jack pulled a couple of pieces of paper from his pocket. "I sent the information to the general advertising email, but I wanted to see what you're printing and my options for streamlining or fixing it."

"You sent it to the online form and email?" Shaun settled on his chair, then rolled up to his desk. "Let me see."

"My assistant did. There should be something from Henry Walters-Lord. He does some freelance work for the paper," Jack said.

"Oh yes. Here." Shaun brought up the ad on his tablet and switched to client view. "Here you go. I haven't met Henry, but I hear his work is good. Now, let me know what you want changed or whatever and I'll do it."

Jack looked over the ad. "Just the name of the shop. It's Jack's Hot Dog Shop. No extra letters—no p or e. We're not that fancy."

"God it." Shaun noted the changes. If he recalled right, the information had been added per the client, but whatever. Maybe Henry wasn't a great typist.

"And we only accept cash, except for the online orders — those can be cash or charge."

"I'll fix that, too." That information should've been noted in the extra information section, but he'd bet the assistant hadn't read that far. Few people did. "How long do you want it to run?"

"A month."

"Done." He noted the information on the paper, then fixed the letters and wording. "Now look at it."

"That's great." Jack sighed. "It's been hectic lately. Henry and I got married, consolidated our homes and I can't keep anything on track outside of the restaurant. It's like my world got turned upside down."

"I hear you — I'm not moving in with anyone. My now ex-boyfriend and I were together for ten years and he refused to commit. I wanted to get married and he wanted to start dating again. It threw my life into flux, so I can't imagine trying to consolidate and get married."

"If you don't mind me asking, what convinced him he should start dating?" Jack massaged his forehead. "It's not my business."

"No, I don't mind. He had a guy on the side, so the dating thing was their idea," Shaun said. "He never wanted to be with one guy for long, but I had no clue he'd been dating people while we were together. I've nicknamed him 'the shark' because he's always got to keep moving."

"Ah, one of those."

"When did you know Henry was the one, since we're discussing such things?" Shaun saved the ad template and moved his tablet aside. "I thought Jonah was the one and I was wrong." He paused. "If you don't mind me asking."

"Don't mind it at all." Jack shifted in his seat. "I knew Henry was the one when he wasn't jealous of the restaurant and wanted to help me. Other guys gave me the choice of them or the shop. I can't dump my business. It's my livelihood. If it's done, then I'm done, and I needed a man who could accept that."

"Makes sense." He turned the tablet around. "This is the final ad. What do you think?"

Jack nodded. "Perfect. Thank you. I did get the bill and it's paid."

"Great. This will go starting tomorrow and will be in the lifestyle section for the first week, then alternate between the sports and national news sections for two weeks. The final week it'll go back to the lifestyle section, but it'll run every day."

"That's exactly what I want." Jack stood. "I've never run an advertisement before and this was painless, so thank you for that. I was worried it'd be difficult or something."

"I try to keep it simple," Shaun said. "I know it's stressful to figure out what to say, where to advertise and how best to spend your money. The nice thing about your month-long ad is that it'll run on the website, too. So you get a little more bang for your buck and we can arrange for a clip to be recorded for the web show."

"You have one?" Jack nodded again. "I had no idea, but I'm not fluent with the Internet. That's Henry's domain."

"I hear you. I thought I was print or nothing, but the web versions are nice." He followed Jack down the hallway. "Is there space to eat in your shop, or is it strictly grab-and-go?"

"To-go is best. It's small, so there's not much room for eating in, but if you know when you'd like to come in, we can have a table available."

"I'll have to keep that in mind. I'm trying to find small places to go with Kevin for dates. Plus, I've got to try what I'm advertising," Shaun said. "Can't say it's great if I don't know personally."

"Kevin?" Jack asked. "Kevin Keiser?"

"Yeah. Do you know him?"

"I do. He worked for me over one summer before college. He's a nice kid, er, guy. Smart, too. He's working for the food services portion of the baseball team." Jack shrugged. "He's the head of food services, I mean. Are you together?"

"We're feeling each other out." They hadn't actually started dating, but he had hope they'd be able to take things to that level. He kept stumbling over himself while trying to ask Kevin out.

"Well, you can't go wrong with Kevin," Jack said. "I hope it works out."

"Me, too." He walked with Jack to the foyer. "Thanks for advertising with us."

"Thanks. Stop by soon and we'll make you something great." Jack waved, then left.

Shaun returned to his office and work, but his thoughts never wandered far from Kevin. God, he was hung up already. He chuckled. It was so like him to do this—get caught up on someone so fast. When he decided he liked someone, he dove in head first.

Shaun finalized the ad for Jack, then called Stone. He wanted to stop by the shelter, too. Ever since he'd come to Cedarwood, he'd debated getting a cat or dog. Kevin had a cat. What if the cat didn't like him? What if the cat loved Kevin and not him? Or what if the cat hated everyone? What if the critter was just what he needed to fill his chilly nights until he found the right guy?

Half an hour later, he'd shored up the details with Stone for the advertisement, plus set up time to meet for photos with the first prospective animal.

His phone rang and he didn't bother to check the ID before he answered. "Hello, this is Shaun Fallows and you've reached the advertising desk for the Cedarwood Tribune, how may I help you?"

"Shaun, this is Kyle — Kyle Beglin." Kyle laughed. "I thought you'd know me."

"I didn't look at the screen." Shaun shook his head. "What can I do for you?"

"What are you doing?" Kyle asked. "This afternoon?"

"Working." Shaun tapped the phone and set it to speaker, then worked on the type for the shelter ad. "You know, doing my job?"

"Okay, fair enough. What are you doing tonight?"

"Getting coffee with a friend." He wished Kyle would get to the point so he could focus on the advertisement.

"Where?"

"I'm not sure because we're still deciding." He retyped the name of the shelter twice before getting it right. *Damn.* He didn't need careless mistakes in this ad. "Does it matter?"

"Yes, it does, because I wanted to meet up."

"Do you need to discuss advertising?"

"No, but you could use a friend in case the date goes sideways," Kyle said.

"How do you know that will happen or that it's a date?"

"I saw you eyeballing Kevin."

"Oh yeah?" Everyone had seen him. He hadn't been shy about his attraction and the folks on the staff at the paper had heard him ask Kevin out. "So?"

"He's…you might want a hasty retreat."

"Let me decide and get back to work. I still have deadlines to meet tonight."

"Sure, but you'll want to call me when it doesn't work out."

"I doubt that. Look, I need to go so I can meet with a client." He was lying, but he didn't care. "See you."

"Shaun."

Shaun hung up on Kyle and switched his phone to vibrate. According to the clock, he had half an hour to finish the ad type for the shelter before printing and he didn't need any more intrusions.

Kyle annoyed him. How could one man be so pushy? Sure, Kyle was attractive, but his attitude and drive were a little intense for Shaun. Besides, why did Kyle need to keep interjecting himself into the situation with Kevin? They were all adults and could handle themselves.

Oh well. Right now, he needed to finish his projects. If he wanted to see Kevin and try to nab an actual date, then he needed to have his work done. Plus, now he had the chance to figure out how to show Kevin a good time.

* * * *

Kevin arrived at the coffee shop early. He liked being ahead of schedule, because then he knew he wouldn't be late. Kyle had called him ridiculous for his need to be on time. *"Arrive late and make a statement,"*

Kyle would say. He disagreed. Being early meant he was prepared.

Joe walked up to Kevin's table. "Hey you. How are things? Want your usual?"

"The usual is good, thank you. I'm meeting someone," he said and shifted in his seat. "Joe?" Why did he have to be so nervous? He'd gone on dates before. This wasn't even a real date. It was coffee.

"Yeah?" Joe sat across from him. "What's up? You look scared to death. About the guy?"

"Kind of." Admitting as much churned his stomach.

"Kyle?" Joe narrowed his eyes. "He's a terrible influence on you and a jerk at that."

"No." Kyle had been a horrible influence in his life. Kyle had expected him to dress in expensive clothes he couldn't afford, to go out to dinner often—another expense not in the budget—and club. He hated the noise and action of the clubs. Plus, Kyle never stuck around.

"Good. You deserve better." Joe laced his fingers together. "What's the issue?"

"I figured you'd say that, but you're right. I do deserve better, but what's bothering me is sort of the guy. He's not Kyle—he's cute, he's polite and we just met. That's the thing. I'm afraid I'm not doing the right thing and I'm going too fast." Kevin balled his hands on his lap. "One minute I think I'm going along just fine and the next, I'm worried I won't be right for this guy."

"Why?"

"All I can think of is how Kyle berated me. I know I'm not a catch in the same way a lot of guys are—I trip over my own feet, I read too much and I'm picky," he said. "I can't buy a date."

"Except this guy seems to like you. If he didn't, he wouldn't have asked you out."

"It's just coffee."

Joe grinned. "There is no such thing as 'it's just coffee'." He chuckled, then held up his hand. "Let me explain. You're a catch and guys should be chasing you to get a date. Kyle said you weren't good enough because he's an ass. Forget him," he said. "Since we've talked, you've mentioned Kyle a couple times. He shouldn't be on your tongue at all. Put him in the rearview mirror."

"Easier said than done." But the right advice.

"I know, but take it from an old pro at holding on to the past, it doesn't help. You'll be lonely and not happy," Joe said. "It sucks."

"You haven't gone looking for someone since Antwan left?" He'd thought Joe had a boyfriend.

"No. I'm too busy." Joe rubbed his hands together. "I should start looking, but I've been out of the pool for so long…I bet I forgot how to swim."

"You don't forget, but it's easy to get rusty."

Joe sighed. "Let me get your coffee while you wait for your guy, but trust me. Forget Kyle and give this one a chance."

"Sure, thanks." Kevin exhaled as Joe left. He should open up and let Shaun in. At least give Shaun a chance. He spotted Shaun across the coffee shop and stood. "Hi." He waved. "Over here."

"Hey." Shaun's eyes lit up and he hurried over. "I thought I'd be early." He hugged Kevin. "Thanks for getting the table. I've never been here before."

Sparks shot along Kevin's arms and heat flowed in his body. He hadn't felt this way in a long time. He wobbled for a split second, then righted himself and sat across from Shaun. "I like to be early, too. I ordered and Joe knows my usual. When he brings it, you can order."

"Great." Shaun turned his phone off, then tucked it into his front pocket. "Thank you."

"You're a gentleman." Kevin switched his gaze between Shaun's pocket and his eyes. "Not many people are okay with having their phone off for even a second. I kept mine on in case you changed your mind or had car trouble or something." He tapped the button to silence his phone and jammed it into his pocket.

"When I'm with a date, I don't answer the phone, but if I had car trouble, I'd let you know. Thanks for the concern." Shaun rested his forearms on the table. "What did you order?"

"Caramel latte macchiato with extra foam," Kevin said. "Joe should be bringing it over soon." He nodded at Shaun. "I appreciate when my dinner date turns off the phone, because it makes me feel like I'm important." He paused. "Here comes Joe. Have you met him? You said you haven't been here before, right?"

"I haven't met him," Shaun said.

Kevin accepted his coffee. "Joe, this is Shaun. Shaun, this is Joe, the proprietor of the Coffee Bar."

"Nice to meet you," Shaun said. "I'll have the same as Kevin and put both on my bill."

"Sure thing." Joe stood behind Shaun and mouthed, *he's cute – good luck.*

Kevin massaged his forehead. At least Joe seemed to be in his corner. His friend was goofy, but helping make the situation less scary. "Do you like macchiato? It can be too strong."

"I haven't met a coffee I didn't like." Shaun fiddled with the sugar packets. "How long have you lived in Cedarwood?"

"All my life. I left during college and returned to work at the ballfield. I wanted to do communications, but I got in with food service and kept moving up, so I stayed." Kevin shrugged. "My communications degree involved writing press releases and such, but I hated it. I like working with my hands and making the food just so, plus it's a puzzle to put together when I have to work on the pricing and expenses."

"I was going to ask why you didn't try working for the paper, but you've got a good reason." Shaun toyed with his napkin. "I'm better at writing than numbers. I can figure up how much it'll cost per word to post an advertisement, but I'd rather write up the ad instead."

Kevin fiddled with his cup, buying time until Shaun's drink arrived. "I wanted to work for the paper. When I was in high school, I thought I might like to be a journalist, but communications seemed like a better bet career-wise and there weren't any openings at the paper when I graduated. Remy's gotten it back on solid ground, but I needed a job then, so I applied at the ballpark. I started off selling hot dogs at one of the stands and moved up from there."

"Nice." Shaun grinned. "I guess they saw your potential."

Joe arrived with Shaun's drink. "If you need anything else, just shout." He winked at Kevin, then left again.

"So you love working at the ballpark?" Shaun asked, then sipped his drink.

"I was one of the few guys working there—no, I was one of the few workers there—that wasn't trying to date a baseball player." Kevin turned his cup around on the plate. "That was it. I didn't want to do a player and I did my job, so I got the promotion."

"Ah." Shaun waggled his head. "You didn't use the team as a dating pool."

"It's how I met Kyle, though, so it's not all good," Kevin said. "It hasn't all been rosy."

Shaun nodded, then sipped his drink again. "Kyle."

"We dated a while, but Kyle demanded I stop working there and he hated my cat. There was a lot more, but he's in the past and I shouldn't have brought him up." *Damn.* He'd pledged to himself to keep Kyle behind him. Still, he had to defend Leo. "He adopted the cat, but Leo didn't like him and Kyle hated it. He wants to be the center of attention, so when he's not, it drives him crazy."

"That's awful."

"Leo's a good cat, but he's picky, which is why we get along." Kevin pressed his lips together. He kept digging himself deeper into trouble. He'd talked too much about the cat and ended up sounding ridiculous.

"I had a dog, but he liked my mother and refused to leave when I moved, so she kept him," Shaun said. "He stayed with her more than me, so it made sense. He keeps her company and she's got someone to dote on, so it works out."

Kevin nodded. He wasn't sure what else to say so he didn't make a fool of himself. *Shit.* He should fill the void instead of letting it get bigger. "What brought you to Cedarwood? Advertising?"

Shaun fiddled with his cup. "About four years ago, I ran a 5k race here in town. I thought the town was great—it's so homey and quiet. I grew up in Las Vegas with the noise and action, but when my folks split and

Mom moved to Cleveland, I followed. Then I ran the race here and fell in love with the town. My boyfriend wanted to live outside of Columbus, so we moved there. When we split, I needed a new start and found the job opening at the paper. It was fate."

"Nice," Kevin said. "You like to run?"

"I do." Shaun grinned and held up his cup. "Do you?"

"There's a great running path at the Metropark. Remy and Bobby run there. I've run the trails, too. The routes are a little daunting, but it's good." He wanted a running partner, but lost his words when he came to suggesting Shaun join him.

"I haven't checked that out, but I will," Shaun said. "Do you run?"

"It breaks up the day and lets me blow off frustration." This time, he'd ask Shaun to come along. He'd do it. Talking to Shaun was easier than he'd expected.

"Oh yeah, I'd run for that reason. Might have to start running mid-afternoon." Shaun drank more of his coffee, and silence enveloped them.

Kevin wasn't sure what to talk about. He couldn't disclose everything right away.

"You asked about why I'm here—besides the race, I thought it might be nice to put down roots. No one knew me here, so I could be myself," Shaun said. He finished his drink and nudged the cup away. "It's nice to not have to play up to an image or be something I'm not."

Kevin stared at him. Shaun was handsome and seemed normal, but the *something he wasn't* comment rankled with him. "Why? Did you have to live up to the

antics of a sibling or did you do something you regret?"
God, he sounded nosy. "I mean…never mind."

"I'm not running from anything, no." Shaun
laughed. "I wanted to buy a house, even though I
haven't yet because there are too many choices and I
don't have any siblings. Just my folks and me. Well, no.
There's my dad and my step-mother, plus my mother."

"Ah." He hadn't bought a home or put down proper
roots, but he also couldn't seem to leave his hometown.
After splitting from Kyle, roots seemed unimportant.

"You seem comfortable here. I've heard stories
about coming out in Cedarwood and it being
dangerous," Shaun said. "It doesn't seem dangerous."

"It used to be. People have sort of simmered down
in the last couple years. The undercurrent of anger is
still there, but it's not at the forefront." Kevin blotted
his mouth with his napkin, then moved his cup to the
side. "When I told my parents I was gay, my mom
hugged me and my dad told me he knew all along.
Neither got upset and they encouraged me to be
myself. It was like a release when I admitted it—I
wasn't hiding and they weren't trying to dance around
it. At school, life wasn't great. I was smart, different and
the kids I graduated with didn't understand how to act
around someone who was gay." He shrugged. "The
town could be rough back then and there is always
someone who wants to be an asshole, but it's not as bad
as it's been."

Kevin suppressed a shudder. He hated talking about
that part of his past and disliked how the town wasn't
as quick to accept everyone as he would've preferred.
Every so often, when he got low, he could still hear
their voices in his ears, reminding him that being
different wasn't cool.

Shaun reached across the table and touched Kevin's hand. "Are you okay?"

"Sometimes the negative moods hit and I get stuck remembering what I went through." Kevin shrugged, but didn't pull away from Shaun. The comfort in Shaun's touch reassured him. "I wasn't the target, but there was a group that would attack the gay community. Like actual attacks. Shit on cars, flaming shit…one guy was assaulted."

"Ouch."

"It's more harmonious now, but you never know."

"Nope."

The volume of noise in the shop increased. Kevin balled his free hand on his lap. As much as he could stand the confusion and action in the stadium, he hated it in smaller spaces like the coffee shop. "It's getting busy and Joe has music on Thursday nights. Sometimes the music is good and other times it's not so much."

"Yikes." Shaun rubbed the top of Kevin's hand with the pad of his thumb. "Why'd you and Kyle split? The cat?"

"Mostly. We were going down different paths and it just wasn't working. Neither of us wanted to put in the effort." No, he'd invested his time and Kyle didn't care. "Kyle wanted everyone to look at him, and when they didn't, he got angry."

"That bothered you. Were you jealous?"

"God, no. I don't care that he attracted attention, but I cared that he ignored me in favor of it." He hated thinking about Kyle and had spent too much time discussing him. "I never mattered. If he could be in the spotlight, he did it."

"I got that impression." Shaun held Kevin's hand. "His loss. You're cute and I'll bet you're both loyal and sweet, too."

"I can be." The comment made him sound like he was a dog, but whatever. Shaun was easy to talk to and Kevin liked the way he held his hand.

"I'd like to see you again. I'm not much of a cook, but how about dinner Saturday? My place, say around six? I'll make food and we can catch a movie." Shaun's eyes glittered.

"You want to with me?" Kevin blurted. He really needed to think before he spoke.

"Who else?"

Duh...him. "I—" When Kevin looked up, Kyle approached the table. "Fuck."

"Oh, good. I fuck, too." An odd smile crossed Shaun's lips. "You look like you've seen a ghost."

Pretty much. Kyle marched over to the table and sat beside Shaun. He draped his arm around Shaun's shoulders. "So this is where you wanted to meet? Quaint." He narrowed his eyes. "Kevin."

Shaun tensed. "Kyle?"

"Right here." Kyle kissed Shaun on the lips. "Missed me?"

"I…" Shaun paled, then met Kevin's gaze. "Sorry."

"Don't be." Kevin let go of Shaun's hand and stood. "I see I'm interrupting. See you around." He left the table without looking back. He'd started developing feelings for Shaun. Granted, Shaun wasn't necessarily his and they weren't a couple, but why did he have to pick Kyle? Kevin shoved his hands into his pockets and walked the four blocks home. He couldn't compete with Kyle for Shaun's attention. Not when Kyle looked like he'd stepped out of a fashion magazine.

He sighed. He liked Shaun and wanted to think running into Kyle was a coincidence, but Christ, he was forty years old and too far gone to waste time with someone who wanted to play around.

One day, the right man would come along and sweep him off his feet.

Just not today.

Chapter Three

Shaun shoved Kyle away and growled. He'd lost perfectly good time with Kevin because Kyle had to be a dick. "What are you doing?" He wiped his mouth and twisted in his seat to see which way Kevin had gone. "I was here with him."

"Waiting on the friend?" Kyle asked. He polished his watch face on his shirt. "Or was he the friend?"

"It's none of your business, but he was the friend, yes." Probably not now. He'd seen Kevin's reaction to Kyle and could feel it, too. Kyle had done a number on him, but what did Shaun expect? Kyle was a toxic person, just like Kevin said. Shaun would be lucky if Kevin spoke to him again.

"Why would you want to meet up with him? Kevin's so boring and he's a server. I work in the offices and have access to the team." Kyle pushed Kevin's empty cup aside. "At least he still has decent taste in coffee. I taught him everything he knows about it."

Shaun sighed and put space between him and Kyle. "I'll bet you did. You molded him into the man he is today, right?" He shook his head. "What did you do? Visit every coffee shop in town until you found me? Stalkerish much?"

"I was making a coffee run and saw you, so I stopped." Kyle shoved another napkin into Kevin's cup. "Why? You looked like you needed rescued."

"I was fine."

"With Kevin?" Kyle crooked his eyebrow. "Really?"

"He's not so bad—not as bad as you think."

"Ah. Not so bad, eh? Translation, he's not fuckable and you're not dying to get him into bed, but you'll give him a pity date. Sounds like you're biding your time." Kyle rolled his eyes. "Oh well. I hear the band is good tonight."

"Might be." Shaun wasn't interested in listening to music tonight, not even his precious Mozart. "I need to go. I've got emails to answer and it's getting stuffy in here."

"My thoughts exactly." Kyle slapped the table. "Let's go."

"You can go anywhere you want. I'm heading home—alone." He put a five-dollar-bill on the table, then stood. "I need to pay the tab."

"He left you with the bill? What an asshole." Kyle snorted. "I wouldn't do that to you."

"It was my treat."

Kyle sighed. "Are you sure you don't want me to come along? I'm great company."

"I'm sure." He left the table. Shaun had thought he'd made some headway with Kevin. Thought they sort of liked each other. Might even be able to start dating. Then Kyle had come along. Jesus Christ. He paid the bill and thanked the girl at the register. "Thanks."

Kyle fell into step beside him out to the lot. "Are you sure you don't want to go somewhere? It's early."

"I had plans and they changed, so no." He stayed by the door of his car. Kyle was too clingy for his tastes.

"Then come with me. We'll hit Sum51 in Cleveland. It's a great club and loaded with hot men. Lots of dancing and music," Kyle said. "You might want to change. Denim is frowned on at the club."

"No thanks." He'd done the clubbing thing and was over it.

"Don't like the music?"

"I'm not in the mood for a concert or dancing tonight." Shaun folded his arms. "But you are, so you should go. Get some of your energy out and have a good time."

"I hate going alone."

"I was here with Kevin and I'm going home alone, so I guess we're even."

"Gag."

His irritation grew. "What did he ever do to you? Huh? You split, and I get that relationships aren't always sweet when they end, but why are you being so nasty?"

"You saw him leave," Kyle said. "He's just not that sexy and he knows it."

"He does?" Kyle wasn't wrong — Kevin's self-esteem appeared to have taken a hit, but with an ex-boyfriend like Kyle, it stood to reason Kevin might be touchy.

"He saw me and bolted. That should tell you everything you need to know," Kyle said. "He can't stand being around me."

"I suppose so." He turned on his heel and walked away. Right now, he needed the space and silence. He rather liked Kevin's awkwardness. He was sweet and, once Shaun got him to open up, Kevin relaxed. Plus, Shaun couldn't help his affinity for men with dark, moody eyes. God, he loved that soulful look. Then there was the phone thing. He'd finally found someone who wasn't glued to their damn cell phone.

He slid behind the wheel of his car and shut the door before Kyle caught up to him. Shaun pressed his phone to his ear and nodded, faking a call. Kyle groaned from his position on the sidewalk, but didn't approach.

Good. He left Kyle in his wake and drove away. *What a nightmare.*

Once he got back to his apartment, he parked in his carport, then headed into his unit. He just wanted a decent date. Not an overly elaborate one, not a club version, but a nice, quiet date where he could get to know the guy — in this case, Kevin.

His phone rang and he checked the ID screen. Cheryl, one of the few friends he still had from the Jonah-era. He set the call to speaker and answered. "Hi, girly."

"Hi, yourself," Cheryl said. "How are things? I see you're settling in. Work's going well? You're posting on social media, which is good. I thought you'd fallen into depression again."

"No, not depressed." He'd left that part of his life behind when he'd moved to Cedarwood. "Things aren't so bad here and I'm getting into the swing of life in the small town. I like my job at the paper, we're getting new advertisements daily and I'm busy, so there's that." He kicked his shoes off. He threw his keys into the basket and abandoned his wallet there, too. "I'm good. You?"

"No, you're not good," she said. "You're miserable."

"No." Not really. "I had a date and it went sideways, but that's life. Honestly, I'm fine."

"A date? With? Dish."

"His name is Kevin. He's a nice guy and has a job, but his ex-boyfriend is persistent. He showed up while we were out and it got awkward."

"Oh no," she said. "Did you come on to the other guy? You flirt without realizing you're doing it."

"I didn't flirt with Kyle. No. He's cute, but it's not anything I want to involve myself with. Plus, he reminds me of Jonah. He wants attention and needs to have a relationship." Shaun shook his head and plopped on the couch. "He's not anything I'm looking for."

"Right. You don't need another Jonah. He sucked the life out of you."

"He did." He hadn't thought about the relationship that way, but she was right. He hadn't been happy with his ex. Miserable was more like it. Nothing had ever pleased Jonah and there wasn't enough money in the world for him.

"What's wrong with Kevin?" Cheryl asked.

"For one, he's intimidated by his ex. Kyle is about as pushy as Jonah and determined, too. Second, he's shy. Like the sexy, sweet, isn't sure about himself and doesn't know he's handsome kind of shy." He crossed his ankles. "Then there are the sparks. When we touched…man. I haven't felt like that in a long time. He's like nothing I've ever experienced and the kind of guy I like. Plus, he's tall, dark and handsome."

"Then why didn't you take him home?"

"If he hadn't beat feet as soon as Kyle showed up, that was the plan." Shaun sighed and rested his head on the back of the cushion. "Remember when you dated Nick and things were fine until Kate showed up and Nick kept leaving? It's like that. Kyle is so damn pushy and overbearing that he forces Kevin to retreat. You can't get a word in edgewise with him."

"Ouch."

"I know."

"You're going to text him, right? And get him to come over?" she asked. "At least set up another date. You have to, and make it up to him."

"That's the plan. I'm going to let Kevin have some space for a day, then I'll text tomorrow." He shook his head. "You didn't see the frantic look in his eyes. Kyle really did a number on him."

"Guys like that do," she said. "So then, you're happy?"

"I am." He sat up. "What about you? Things are settling down?"

"For the most part. I got Giorgio to commit and we're talking about a July wedding," she said. "But we'll see. I haven't gotten a ring yet."

"Don't push him. That'll only make him dig in deeper." Shaun laughed. He appreciated their chats. She knew how to ground him in ways only a friend could, plus, there wasn't the undercurrent of sexual tension. They took each other at face value.

"You'll come down to Columbus soon, won't you? We miss you." She sighed. "Bring that boy of yours. He sounds yummy."

"If I can get Kevin to forgive me, then I'll try," he said. "Thanks for checking in on me."

"Of course. We have to make sure each other is okay," she said. "Now, give that boy of yours a kiss and tell him a date is in order. Sex him up, too."

"Cheryl." He laughed. "We'll set up something to come visit."

"Deal. I want to meet this guy who has you all twisted up. Sounds like a keeper," she said. "Love you."

"Love you." He hung up and closed his eyes. She'd cheered him out of his funk, at least.

His thoughts turned to Kevin. Shaun had to look at the situation differently. Kevin was shy and needed to feel safe. Shaun could do that. He'd try anything to get Kevin to open up again—even if it meant they were only meant to be friends. But the spark came to mind. There was a crackle between him and Kevin. This wasn't a friends-only thing.

He'd work to convince Kevin to give him a try. With his heart on the line, he had no other choice.

* * * *

Saturday afternoon, Shaun checked the team calendar one more time. The game today was going along according to the schedule—no big delays. *Good.* The matchup between Cedarwood and Ridgeville was probably the reason Kevin hadn't returned any of Shaun's texts, too. Being busy and working tended to impede on texting time. Then again, Kevin could still be pissed, too.

Shaun stared at his closet and debated his choices. He could keep trying to text Kevin and possibly give up, or he could go to the stadium and see him.

A surprise seemed in order.

Shaun showered, then dressed in one of his favorite college T-shirts, the garment that showcased his biceps. He selected a pair of butter-soft jeans. Once he'd styled his hair and donned a pair of socks, he located his favorite pair of cowboy boots. The footwear might be a bit much, but if he was going to go for sexy, he might as well play to his strengths.

He checked his look in the mirror—sexy, but not desperate. *Good.* He tucked his phone into his pocket, grabbed his keys and wallet, then left. If nothing else, he'd get answers.

Shaun drove to the stadium, listening to Mozart. He needed grounding today like no other. Once he reached the lot, he wondered where Kevin would park and what kind of car he drove. *Fuck.* Who would know this stuff?

Cara might. He dialed her number and turned the music down. After two rings, she answered.

"Hi," she said. "What do you need?"

"You know Kevin, right? What kind of car does he drive? I want to surprise him."

"A Subaru. A boring four-door car." She paused. "What's the surprise?"

"I wanted to see him when he got off work."

"You're coming on a bit strong. You might freak him out."

"I know, but I need to do something big to fix my mistake," Shaun said. He located the staff lot and the lone Subaru. "I think I found it."

"What mistake?" she asked.

"Just trust me and I'll tell you Monday, but it was a big one."

"Okay, but look for a blue four-door," she said. "Tell me what you're going to do, so if I have to put the brakes on, I can."

"I'm going to do the best I can." He parked next to Kevin's car and turned his engine off. "Thanks, and I'll talk to you Monday. Wish me luck and I promise to tell you everything then, okay?"

"Luck."

He hung up. According to the schedule, the game had just ended. People were filing out of the stadium, so the timing must be correct. How long would food service have to stick around afterward? An hour?

If nothing else, he had time to sort out the next part of his plan.

He arranged his hair and admired himself in the mirror. "Here goes nothing."

* * * *

Kevin locked up the kitchen and headed down the corridor to the employee exit. His back ached from being hunched over the fryer for the last hour of the ballgame. He massaged his lower back, then stopped at his locker long enough to retrieve his keys, ruined personal phone, work phone and wallet. *God.* Nothing had gone right. He'd had to toss a case of stale buns and the taps on two of the kegs had broken, not to mention his personal phone. *How could so much have gone haywire?*

At least Kyle hadn't stopped him.

He headed out of the building and into the waning sunshine. Most of the cars were gone from the lot, but one had parked right next to his. A man stretched out on the hood of the car. The closer he got to the vehicle, he realized the guy on the car wasn't just anyone.

Shaun.

Kevin wanted to hide, but why? He liked Shaun, and despite the disaster the other day, he longed to see him again. "Hi."

"Hi." Shaun sat up and adjusted his sunglasses. "You're done?"

"I am." He swept his gaze over Shaun. The jeans and shirt fit like a second skin. Hell, he could be prepping for a photo shoot in this outfit. He reminded Kevin of the calendars with the boy-next-door models. Shaun could be one. Kevin's mouth watered and he wondered what Shaun's kiss might taste like.

Kevin ventured over to Shaun. "You'll chip your paint sitting on it. Your pocket rivets will scratch it."

Shaun shrugged. "I won't do too much damage." He scooted to the front of the hood and slid until his feet were planted on the asphalt. "You haven't answered my texts and I wanted to apologize."

Kevin held up his hand. "Slow down." If he wanted a chance with Shaun, he needed to stop being scared. Shaun was just a guy—like him—a human. "I didn't answer the texts because I haven't gotten them. My phone is slow and it's even worse now since I dropped it in a sink of hot water."

"Ouch." Shaun grasped Kevin's right hand. "Bricked it?"

"Completely." He allowed Shaun to tug him forward until he settled against the vee of his legs. "I got a couple texts from you, I think, but by the time I had a chance to read them, I'd ruined the phone. Once I get out of here, I'm going to get a new one."

"Do you need it? Like can you go until tomorrow before you replace it?" Shaun held both of Kevin's hands. "Or will something come to a crashing end if you don't?"

He still had his work phone and anything of importance would come across that one. "It could wait."

"Yeah?"

"Yeah." Kevin swept his gaze over Shaun again. "I love the effect you're going for here. I've never had a hot guy waiting for me to finish work."

"You think I'm hot?" Shaun's mouth curled in a wicked grin.

"I do," Kevin said, his voice husky and almost unrecognizable. "But how long were you out here?"

"I confess, it's been almost an hour." Shaun blushed and let go of Kevin's hands long enough to encircle him in his embrace. "I wasn't sure how long it'd take for you to come out, so I played it safe and arrived early. I've only been on the hood for about ten minutes, and I'm glad it's a somewhat cloudy day, or my hide would be toast."

"It would." Kevin sighed. He should explain his hasty retreat at the Coffee Bar. "I'm sorry I freaked out and left the other day."

"Will you tell me why?"

He screwed up his courage. Admitting the truth wasn't all that bad and he liked the way Shaun held him. "It's Kyle. He has a knack for getting involved in my life when I think he's out. I think I'm in the clear and he shows up to wreck stuff."

"He's done it before."

"Twice with potential boyfriends and all the time at work." He hated the way the truth sounded, like he was helpless. "I'm working on not letting it bother me. Right after the breakup, it was bad, but I have a job to do and I want to do it."

"But he likes to show up when you're not in a controlled environment?"

Shaun understood? "Yeah, and his actions make life difficult."

"I'm not shocked." Shaun groaned. "And he's coming over." He kept his hold on Kevin. "What he doesn't understand is that I don't care. I went out with you and I'm here for *you*—not him." He squeezed Kevin's ass. "I like your crooked smile, the way your eyes light up when you grin and that you have a nice ass."

"I do?" He'd never given much thought to his own ass.

"You do," Shaun murmured.

Before Shaun could say more, Kyle approached. "Kevin. Shaun." He stood beside them. "To what do I owe this pleasure?"

Kevin steeled himself for the onslaught of negative comments. He hadn't been as interested in other guys in the way he was with Shaun and he didn't want Kyle's intrusion. "I don't know what you owe it to."

"I'm not here for you," Shaun said. He never took his gaze off Kevin. "I came for other reasons."

"This isn't a social club, gentlemen," Kyle said and nudged Shaun. "You're acting childish."

"But if I were here for you, it'd be a different story," Shaun said. He tugged Kevin closer. "It's no different than a guy meeting his gal after work or two women meeting…or two friends, even. He asked me to join him and I did."

Kevin nodded. He wasn't letting Kyle take this moment from him. "I did."

"Right. You've never had this much backbone in your life," Kyle snapped. "Stop." He held up both hands. "I get it. You did this to make me jealous. Well, it worked. I'm jealous. Now, Shaun, ditch him so we can go."

"Nope." Shaun brushed his nose along Kevin's enough that his breath tickled Kevin's cheek. "I'm good."

"So am I." Kevin bridged the gap between them and kissed Shaun. This wasn't how he'd planned on their first kiss going, but he craved Shaun's kiss. Besides, the perfect moment, whatever that might be, wasn't everything. He needed the right push and his lips on Shaun's worked. He liked the feel of Shaun's breath on his skin, the way Shaun massaged his ass as they kissed. He caressed Shaun's shoulders and closed his eyes while he enjoyed this moment. The passion between him and Shaun was palpable. It could be lust, but he didn't care.

"Enough." Kyle swatted Kevin's arm. "Hey. I said enough."

Kevin broke the kiss and stared into Shaun's eyes. The crystal blue intoxicated him.

"You can go now," Shaun said. He kept Kevin in his embrace.

"I thought we were together," Kyle growled. "You told me we were."

This time, Shaun bristled. "I said nothing of the sort. You assumed and it looks like you're just saying this to cause trouble."

"Well." Kyle stomped his foot. "See if I take you clubbing again. Good evening."

Again? Kevin kept his poise, but not by much. *Jesus.* Kyle insisted on butting into everything.

When Kyle walked away, Kevin exhaled and Shaun sighed. "I guess we both have a bit of confession coming," Shaun said. "I never asked him out—for coffee or clubbing, but I was polite to him because the paper does advertising for the team."

"I knew." Kevin put some space between him and Shaun. "You said something about dinner tonight. Well, before everything went to hell. Are you still interested? We can order something out."

"We could." Shaun's eyes glittered. "My place or yours?"

"Either." He had no preference. "Mine's just small and my cat will want to get in your face. He's pushy."

"I can handle pushy. I've dealt with Kyle." Shaun hooked his fingers in Kevin's front pockets. "Why don't we go to yours so you can shower and change? I'll handle dinner and get to know your cat."

"I'd like that." Kevin brushed his hand over Shaun's arm. "You'll follow me?"

"I will."

He kissed Shaun again and electricity sizzled between them. His lips tingled and his heart beat faster. When he pulled back a bit, his breath caught in his throat. For once he was happy. This handsome man liked him. This one. God, he was lucky. He caressed Shaun's forearm. "Did you spray paint your pants on?"

"Just about." Shaun chuckled. "They're my favorites."

"I can tell." He liked the way Shaun looked in the denim. "We should get going. My stomach is going to start rumbling soon, and no one wants to hear that. Besides, the cat will want feeding and he can be a pain in the ass until he gets his dinner."

Shaun shrugged. "It happens. So, where are you at? Which place is yours?"

"I'm in the Harrington Building," Kevin said. "It's on First Avenue."

"I know where that is and I'll follow you." Shaun let go. "I like looking at your ass."

The tips of his ears burned. He had no words, but managed to round the hood and locate his keys. He pointed to the exit.

"I'll follow." Shaun grinned. "I'm right behind you."

"Yeah." *Holy shit.* He slid behind the wheel. Once he left the lot, he checked a couple times to make sure Shaun was indeed a car-length back. The whole situation could be a dream. Guys like Shaun weren't in his league, but Shaun seemed interested.

Hot damn.

Once he drove across town to his apartment building, he parked in the potholed lot and waited for

Shaun as he parked. "This is my place," Kevin said. "I'm on the second floor. It's boring, but it's home."

"Lead the way." Shaun fell into step beside him. "And I doubt it's boring."

"It's not expensive or fancy." He headed into the building to the main staircase. "Up here."

Shaun stayed right with him. "I thought about this complex, but Cara suggested the Wainwright Estates. The only thing that has to do with estates with that place is the name."

"I looked into those, but there weren't any units open and these accepted pets." He strode up to his door. "This is me." He paused. "The cat's name is Leo and he's a pushy orange baby. He doesn't take kindly to some people, but if you let him come to you and don't swat at him, he'll probably like you." He unlocked the door and moved out of the way to let Shaun in first. "It's simple, like I said, but it's home." He didn't know the first thing about interior design, but he liked 'clean and efficient', mostly because he hated cleaning. He spotted Leo lounging on his cat tree and staring at the intruder.

"I like it." Shaun stayed by the door as Kevin entered. "Shoes on or off?"

"Off." He didn't want to be a pain, but he'd always taken his shoes off when he entered the apartment.

"Good. I prefer sock foot at home, too." Shaun closed the door and removed his boots, then touched Kevin's arm. "I know you're scared, but it's okay. I won't bite. Your cat might, but I won't."

Leo sat up and stretched, then let out a growl before departing the cat tree. He narrowed his eyes and sauntered up to Shaun.

Kevin put his wallet, work phone and keys down. He hadn't thought his tensing was visible, but it must've been. "Sorry." He dropped to one knee and scratched Leo behind the ears. "Leo, this is Shaun. Shaun, this is Leo. He rules the roost."

"Hi, Leo." Shaun knelt next to Kevin and placed his open palm on his lap. "You're a good kitty, aren't you?"

Leo stared at him, then sat next to Kevin. His tail swished as he licked his chops. Shaun didn't move, giving the cat a chance to adjust. Leo curled his paw and licked out his toes, then sneezed and stared at Shaun again.

"Am I passing the test?" Shaun mumbled. "Or is he still going to pounce?"

Kevin resumed scratching Leo behind the ears. "He's deciding. You haven't grabbed at him, which is good. He-who-shall-not-be-named used to swat at him."

Shaun offered his fingers, allowing the cat to sniff him. "No need to swat at you." When Leo didn't pull away, Shaun petted his back.

Leo arched his spine and thrust his ass in the air, then whipped his tail and walked away.

"What was that?" Shaun asked. "He vibrated."

"He's always done that. It's his tail thing." Kevin shrugged. "He didn't bite you, so consider yourself lucky. He hasn't accepted you yet, but you're on the right track."

"I can handle that." Shaun grasped Kevin's fingers. "He-who-shall-not-be-named did a number on you and that was crap. Seems like he did a number on Leo, too, but I'm not him. Give me a chance? Please? Looks like Leo's considering it."

Kevin let go and shifted enough to remove his shoes, then grasped Shaun's hand, linking their fingers as he sat on the floor. "I'm trying."

"And I'm patient."

Kevin nodded. "I can work with that." A whole new Chapter of his life seemed to be opening and not a moment too soon. "As for Leo, time will tell, but you're starting out right."

"Good." Shaun squeezed Kevin's fingers, then stood. "What's your poison? I'll order."

"Nothing fried." He needed to wash the scent of grease off his body. He left the floor and tugged his shirt from his pants. "Pizza would be good, or Chinese. I don't care as long as it's not burgers, hot dogs or French fries."

"Nothing you're allergic to?"

"Nope." He didn't pull away from Shaun when he tugged him close. "Unless you're going to feed me eggplant. I'm not wild about eggplant."

"No today." Shaun chuckled. "I'll surprise you."

"Deal." Kevin hesitated before pulling away. "Let me put Leo's food in his bowl, then I'll shower and be right back." He should give Shaun the remote or something. Maybe open his laptop to watch a show? "I don't have cable, but I have TV on my computer, if you want to watch something." He ventured into the kitchen and opened one of the cans of wet cat food. Leo curled around his ankles and bit the top of Kevin's foot. Kevin dished the food into the bowl. "Leo." He placed the dish on the placemat on the floor. "Dinner."

The cat needed no invitation. He settled in front of his food and noshed away happily. Shaun stood at the edge of the room, giving Leo space.

"He's happy when he's eating." Kevin shrugged again. "Did you pick something?"

"I'm going to order food, so don't worry about me unless you're planning on being in the bathroom for hours. I think I know what we'll have, so there's that." Shaun curled his fingers under Kevin's chin. "I'm not high maintenance. I promise." When Kevin turned, Shaun swatted him on the backside. "Go. I'll be fine. Maybe Leo and I will hit it off. You never know."

"I suppose so." He left the warmth of Shaun's touch and ducked into the bathroom. Part of him wasn't sure leaving Leo and Shaun alone together was a good idea. If Leo got spooked or annoyed, he'd bite. Then again, he might climb onto his cat tree and just stare at Shaun. If Shaun didn't pursue Leo and let the cat come to him, he'd be fine.

Kevin turned his attention to his shower. The apartments were designed so the bathroom seemed to be part of the bedroom, but the dual doors meant someone could go into the bathroom via the bedroom or via the living room. It was good for ducking into the bathroom to change, but could make for an embarrassing moment if someone didn't know there was another person in the bathroom.

Oh well. He doubted Shaun would tiptoe into the bathroom to watch him get cleaned up. He probably had his hands full with the cat.

Kevin fought the urge to peek in on Shaun. Instead, he turned the shower on and stripped in minutes. He should take his time, but he wanted to be out in the living room with Shaun. He stepped into the stall and scrubbed his body clean, then washed his hair. He preferred smelling like himself, rather than the stadium.

He rinsed, then hurried right back out of the shower to dry off. He caught sight of his reflection in the condensation-ringed mirror. Were those grays blooming at his temples? Crinkles around his eyes? Did the slight changes matter? He'd spent too much time alone and too much time trying to hide. He needed someone who didn't care if he'd been a bit weathered with age.

Kyle had broken his heart and spirit, but it was time to build them back up.

He should move on, and since Shaun was so tempting, why not move on with him?

He turned the water off and wrapped the towel around his hips. He wished he hadn't gone through the shit with Kyle, but going through it made him appreciate now more. Yeah, he should take a chance with Shaun. This could be the start of something great.

He dressed in jeans and a T-shirt, then padded barefoot out to the living room. "Hi." *Where's the cat and is Shaun bleeding?* "Everything okay?"

"We're fine. Look at you." Shaun left the sofa. Leo sat across the back of the couch and swished his tail. Shaun trailed his fingers down Kevin's front. "I almost didn't recognize you without the stadium outfit. You're handsome when you're being yourself." He wrapped his arms around Kevin. "I like this look."

"Do you?" He swayed with Shaun. "I've always thought I was boring."

"You thought wrong." Shaun trailed his hands along Kevin's ribs. "I don't usually make a bold move when I meet a guy. I like to bide my time and feel him out."

"You're feeling me out pretty well." He rubbed the growing bulge in his pants against the one in Shaun's jeans. The heat engulfed him. He rested his forehead against Shaun's and swayed with him. If he wanted to, he could kiss him. He should.

Shaun cupped Kevin's jaw in both hands. Without a word, he kissed Kevin.

So good. He threaded his arms around Shaun's waist and tucked his hands into his back pockets. His thoughts blurred and all he could do was feel. *Christ.* He'd never been this swept away before. He wanted to rip his clothes off and drag Shaun into his bedroom. He yearned to be with this man. *Craved* him. He wanted to lick every inch of him, then feel Shaun inside him. *Oh God.* He grabbed the front of Shaun's shirt and pressed his body to Shaun's. Yes, this was the time to take this to the next level. He twined his tongue with Shaun's and tasted him. He fumbled Shaun backward until he pinned him to the wall between the bedroom and living room. Shaun overwhelmed him and he loved it.

A buzzer sounded and interrupted the kiss. Shaun broke the connection and rested his forehead on Kevin's. "That would be dinner. Let me go get it."

"Take my keys." Kevin both thanked and cursed the delivery person. He cursed the person because he didn't want the kiss to end, but thanked God he had a moment to think before he got completely caught up. He wasn't the type of person to do what he didn't mean, but he'd almost ripped Shaun's clothes off.

"Be right back, but you don't have to worry about me and Leo. I think we're going to be buds." Shaun took the keys and put his boots on, then left Kevin alone in the apartment.

Kevin fixed his shirt and hair. When he caught sight of himself in the mirror, he grinned. His cheeks were flushed and his eyes wild. He barely recognized himself.

He composed his thoughts, then crossed the room to the sofa and scratched Leo behind the ears. "Are you being nice to our guest or are you just biding your time until you can rip his face off?" He peered into the cat's eyes. "You were good?"

Leo snorted, then tucked himself into a ball, ignoring Kevin.

"Well, okay." Kevin sighed. He'd grown used to the cat's snippy attitude. It was just part of the quirks of Leo.

He glanced at the coffee table. The notion hadn't occurred to him to ask what Shaun had ordered and he had no idea what to prepare for — did they need plates and silver? He grabbed napkins and cleared off the space.

Shaun returned a moment later. "Ready?" He held two paper bags. "I went with Chinese. Got a little of everything. Some soup, egg rolls, rice and chicken. I hope it'll do. I figured Leo's eaten, so it's our turn."

"It is." He grabbed two bowls. "I haven't had Chinese in forever. Oh, and don't expect me to eat with chopsticks. I haven't mastered them, no matter how much I try — and I've tried." He tended to wear more than he ate when he used the implements.

"I've never tried." Shaun placed the bags on the coffee table, then spread the various boxes and cartons out.

Kevin sat across from him on the floor. The food smelled delicious and he offered a napkin. Leo, roused from his momentary nap, strutted over to them and sat on the sofa, watching Kevin.

"Thank you. Help yourself. Leo, you'll have to wait until next time." Shaun dished out rice and chicken. "You're sure this is good enough, Kevin?"

"It's perfect." He waited for Shaun to finish. "I haven't had decent Chinese food in ages. I've suffered through the canned stuff because it was cheaper, but it's not as good."

"Not great at all."

"No." He dished out a portion of rice and chicken. "Thanks."

Leo reached forward and batted at the chopsticks. He knocked one packet on the floor. "Thanks, Leo," Kevin said. "Sorry."

"He's not hurting anything." Shaun held up his bowl. "To us."

"To us." A thought occurred to him. *Shit.* He should get them something to drink. "I'm sorry. What do you want to drink? I have milk, water and a six pack—I think. I had one. I don't drink much and I can't remember when I even bought the beer."

"Water is great." Shaun remained on the floor. "Thank you."

Kevin scrambled to his feet and poured two glasses of water. "Here you go." He returned to the kitchen long enough to retrieve a couple kitty treats for Leo. "And for you."

"To us." Shaun held up his glass.

"You've said that." He laughed. "To this beginning." He placed the treats on the floor and stroked Leo's back while the cat ate.

"Yes." Shaun downed some of the water. "So, Kevin Keiser, what is your ultimate date? If you were told you could go on that date, all expenses paid, what would it be?"

"You mean, what does it consist of?" Kevin asked. He continued to pet the cat.

"Yes." Shaun ate and left the question between them.

"Well…" He had to think about this a bit. "My ultimate date involves me and the guy I'm with, but it's simple. It's easy. A bottle of wine, popcorn maybe and a movie. We'd set up a blanket on the grass and watch a movie in the back yard. Just the two of us. We'd watch the film—probably a black and white one—and cuddle, totally engrossed in each other. The movie doesn't matter because it's really just noise, but we'd be tangled together and happy."

Shaun's odd grin returned. He placed his fork on the bowl. "You're serious?"

Fuck. The tips of his ears burned again. "Yes?" He tamped down his embarrassment. He'd answered wrong. "Why are you looking at me like I've grown horns? It's a simple date idea, but it's too simple for you, isn't it?" He paused. "Are you weirded out by the cat? He's harmless. Snobby, but harmless."

"Marry me," Shaun said. His eyes widened. "Whoa."

"Wait. What?" He must've heard Shaun wrong. "Did you say…?"

"I did." Shaun blushed, then covered his face with his hands. "That slipped out."

"Oh." He hadn't meant what he'd said. *Okay.* Kevin wished he had. He wanted to find the man he'd marry and start their relationship instead of wasting time.

"Let me clarify," Shaun said. "It was a total slip."

He should've guessed. So much for hoping Shaun might be the one.

"But what I said wasn't entirely wrong." Shaun reached across the table and held Kevin's hand. "If I were planning my ultimate date, it's almost a carbon copy of yours. We'd have the movie showing from a projector or one of those fancy projection things, but shown on a sheet. We'd have a little fire, too." He chuckled. "No one ever came close to having the same kind of ultimate date."

"I said I'm simple." And he liked the way Shaun thought. "I have a clingy cat and I'm not handsome like some guys."

"Your simple is sexy." Shaun rubbed the top of Kevin's hand. "You keep intriguing me. You say the right things, even when you think you're wrong. In doing that, you seem to know what I like and you're my kind of man. I even like the cat, and until today, I wouldn't have considered myself a cat person. I guess Leo's winning me over."

"And that's what made you make the statement about marriage?" Kevin stared at him. He liked the honesty and homey feeling between them. *Like we could be a couple.*

"Sort of," Shaun said. "I told my friend Cheryl that when I found the guy whose idea of the ultimate date meshed with mine — it consisted of being together and not about spending disgusting amounts of money — I'd marry him."

"And you know after one date with my cat monitoring everything, one botched date where my ridiculous ex showed up, and my description, that I'm the one?" Kevin smiled, but the idea of marrying Shaun wasn't far-fetched. A little fast, but not impossible. He could see forever in Shaun's eyes.

"Yeah."

Kevin held Shaun's hand tighter. "We need time to let this — us — happen. To grow. You can't know I'm the one that fast."

"Why not?" Shaun's smile widened. "I could know. I've got friends who fell in love quite fast and knew within days. It's possible."

"But we've both thought we were in love before and got it wrong. What if this time is no different? What if…" He could come up with a hundred excuses.

"What if we make it?"

The idea both scared and intrigued him. "Yeah."

"I didn't say we were riding off into the sunset together with Leo tonight," Shaun said. "I can't even stay over tonight. I'm due at the newspaper office at seven. If I stay tonight, no one will get any sleep and I won't make it to work on time. Leo might not appreciate having to stay up all night listening to us, either."

Holy hell. Shaun was thinking along the lines he'd arrived at, too. "Leo won't care."

Shaun ate in silence, but his smile remained. Kevin finished his dinner, but wasn't sure what to say. The confession and Shaun's proclamation hung heavy in the air.

Shaun balled up his napkin. "I know I keep rushing the situation and I'm overly excited. I want this to work, and if you want us to take time to get to know each other, then that's what we'll do, because I agree."

Kevin liked the way he thought.

"But I have a few…rules? That's not the right word, but I can't come up with the correct one."

"Conditions?" Kevin asked. "Like getting rid of Leo? That's a non-starter."

"Nothing like that." Shaun laced his fingers together and propped his chin on his knuckles. "Do you want to be a couple?"

"With you?" He'd blurted the wrong thing. *Damn it.*

"With me."

"Yes." He had no hesitation—once he got clarification. He'd started falling for Shaun the moment they'd discussed the date. "Do you?"

"Yes," Shaun said. "Next one. Since we're doing this, we aren't doing anyone else. Does that make sense?"

"It does. You're saying you want to be exclusive."

"I know it sounds shitty, but if you're with me, then we're with each other. No one else," Shaun said. "I'm too old to play games."

Kevin snorted. "You're not old. You're, what, thirty-four? That's not old."

"I'm forty-two."

"You don't look it." He'd aged quite well.

"And you?"

"I'm forty." *Oh God.* "I think I'm careening headlong into old man mode with my cat and my solitude."

"No, you're not, and neither of us looks our age." Shaun exhaled. "Whoa."

"Are you okay? You said that before." Kevin inched around the coffee table and sat beside Shaun. "Shaun?" The cat curled on the couch cushion, ignoring him and Shaun. "Leo's leaving us alone."

"No, I'm...it's..." Shaun frowned. "I don't want to mess this up. I like you and I want to be with you, but I guess I'm clumsy at relationships. I dove in too fast and I'm worried you're going to put the brakes on, since I can't. As for Leo, he's fine."

Kevin scooted closer and bumped knees with Shaun. "I'm a fumbler and you are, too, so we fumble through this together. It won't be easy all the time, but I don't want to go through this journey alone." He kissed Shaun. "You're the one I want with me."

Shaun kissed him hard. "I so want to stay over."

"I've got to work, too," Kevin said. "But this gives us time. When are you free to get together next?"

"Mondays are my long days. We have to set up the ad pages for the week all at once." Shaun crawled onto Kevin's lap and straddled him. "Tuesday?"

"I've got inventory tomorrow," Kevin said. "There's a game on Tuesday, too." He patted Shaun's ass. "Up. I need to clean up the mess." Not that he didn't want Shaun to stay put. He did. "If I don't toss this stuff, the cat will get into it, and we don't want to clean that up."

"No, we don't." Shaun helped collect the garbage and dispose of it. "I'm done at noon on Wednesday. I could meet you. After work?"

"How about lunch? The food trucks in town are dangerously good." Kevin wiped his hands on a towel. "Then we can sit in the park in the center of town." He liked going there and watching the people move around the square.

"I love it."

Kevin pinned Shaun to the cabinets in the kitchen and kissed him. He and Shaun were at the beginning of something fantastic. He couldn't wait for their next date. He'd found a guy who didn't mind the cat, had manners and was freaking sexy. "We're doing this?"

"We are." Shaun brushed his nose along Kevin's and sighed. "We so are."

Kevin held his boyfriend tight. His life was finally going in the right direction. *Thank you, God.*

Chapter Four

Shaun practically skipped through his day on Monday. His heart was light and his spirits soared. He had a boyfriend and was happy. For the first time in a long while, he knew where he stood with his man and had no worries. Granted, he wished he could've stayed with Kevin and explored every inch of his sexy body, but he appreciated Kevin's desire to slow down.

God. He needed to rein himself in. When he looked at Kevin, he wanted to strip him and fuck him until they couldn't walk.

Good thing that Kevin was thinking straight for the both of them.

Shaun forced himself to focus on his work. He adjusted the copy on Thursday's ad page, then stood back to admire his work.

"Looks good." Remy Nicholas stood beside him. "You're a whiz with this stuff. I write, but I can't arrange for shit. Ask Bobby. He'll tell you I made a mess of the photo collage he had on the wall in the den. He had to fix it."

"Thanks." He liked arranging and placing the ads. Plus, he had proper spacing for everything. "I read your editorials. They're good."

"Yeah? I never feel they're done." Remy adjusted two of the boxes of advertising. "I'm going to put you on the pet story, by the way."

"Pet story?" Shaun froze. He wasn't a reporter. "What are you talking about?"

"You're going to interview Stone McCartney for a feature on the animal shelter and you'll get photos of the animals. You'll be in charge of working with him to pick the pet of the week." Remy folded his arms. "You'll be great at it."

"I'm advertising, not copy writing." He hadn't written a proper story in forever. "I'll screw it up."

"I doubt that." Remy widened his stance. "We're in the black, but I see more for you and I think you're up for this. You're good. This, arranging and writing up ads, is easy. You could do it in your sleep."

Maybe.

"And you're doing well with publishing for the paper. I liked your idea of putting a small feature section in for the stories about the baseball team. Daron's idea to create a special free paper to distribute at the park is good, too," Remy said. "I want both meshed so we can entice people at the stadium to become subscribers."

He'd forgotten all about the feature thing he'd suggested.

"I'm putting Daron on interviewing the players," Remy said. "He'll be contacting a Kyle Beglin. You know him, right?"

"Too well." *And not in a good way.*

"You're seeing him?" Remy narrowed his eyes.

"No." *Gross.* "I'm seeing Kevin Keiser. It's new, but we're in a good place."

"Nice. I believe he went to school with Bobby," Remy said. "Might not have been in the same graduating class."

He had no idea, but he wasn't about to argue.

"Anyway, if you can connect Daron with Kyle, that would be great. It'll jumpstart the interview process," Remy said. "And will get him off my back. Daron wants to work with the team and I have the feeling he's trying to get a job with them."

"Might be." He didn't listen to the gossip around the office and had no idea. But, if he could get Daron and Kyle together and redirect Kyle's attention from Kevin, then great. "Anything else?"

"Nope." Remy clapped him on the shoulder. "Are you happy here? In Cedarwood?"

He nodded. "I thought I wouldn't be, but it's gotten better. I met Kevin and we're trying a relationship, so there's that," Shaun said. "It's nice to have someone and we're serious enough that we're exclusive, but still meeting for dates. I like knowing we're on the same page and I even met his cat. We're chummy." Well, as chummy as he could be with a feline after one meeting. "Plus, I feel like I belong."

"You do." Remy started away from him, then stopped short. "Hey. We're a sponsor for the upcoming 5k race. I know you run and I've seen Kevin run on the trails at the Metropark. Would you be interested in running the race and wearing a *Tribune* shirt to be a moving advertisement?"

"I signed up for it." He should ask Kevin if he wanted to run it, too. "When is the deadline? I don't remember."

"I'm fairly sure it's passed, but don't worry about it. I've got shirts for you, me, Bobby, Chris, a few others and Kevin, if he's interested." Remy rested his hands on his hips. "Think Kevin would be interested in wearing a *Tribune* shirt for the race?"

"He might, but he might feel conflicted, too—if he wants to run it." He should ask Kevin and not expect he'd comply.

"True." Remy nodded. "Well, ask him if he'd like to do it and I'll ensure everyone is registered. Thanks. Team *Tribune*!"

Shaun snorted. *Team Tribune?* The name sounded silly, but also kind of cool. He belonged and now he had Kevin, too.

Right now, he needed to get back to work. He finished the mock-ups and sent them to the printer for the final checks.

Plus, he wanted a break for supper. He headed to his office and closed the door. He picked up his cell phone and typed a text to send to Kevin.

Hey you. Hope work is going okay. On dinner break and wanted to say hi. Miss you.

He hit Send before he could second-guess himself. He rather liked the pace the relationship was going and Kevin's need to slow down. With most other relationships, Shaun jumped right into bed and the fire spiraled out of control—usually on a fast course to dying out. Not so with Kevin. They had time to figure out what they wanted and keep the fire stoked.

His phone buzzed. He checked the ID screen. Kevin calling. His heart hammered as he answered. "Hi."

"Hi," Kevin said. "I'm on a break, so instead of texting, I thought I'd call. How's work?"

"Good. We finalized most of the ads and we'll check the print versions after dinner, but it's good," he said. The 5k came to mind. "We're sponsoring the race in September. Just found out."

"Nice," Kevin said. "Do you have to help with it? Man a table or something?"

"I've been asked to run it and wear a shirt with the paper's logo on it," Shaun said. "I planned to run it anyway."

"Good. Those are fun."

He hesitated. "Are you going to do it?"

"The race?"

"Yeah."

"It's past the time to sign up or I would. I wanted to make sure we didn't have a game that day and I forgot to register."

"Are you serious? Do you really want to run it?" Shaun asked.

"I do, and I'd like to run it with you."

"I can get you signed up." He'd pull strings with Remy and have it done by the end of the day.

"Thanks. That'd be awesome," Kevin said. "I appreciate it. We need to get to practicing or we'll be rusty—I will anyway. I haven't gone for a run in five days."

"Run with you? Oh darn. Gotta spend time together and run." Shaun laughed. "I'm looking forward to it."

"Me, too," Kevin said. "I should go. It's getting crazy here again and Nedra just waved at me. The team is losing, and when they're not playing so well, we tend to sell more food."

Shaun leaned back in his seat and propped his feet on his desk. "Ah, the fans. I never got a chance to ask about your work. Bad Shaun. I hope it evens out and you get to have another break."

"Me, too." Kevin laughed and the line crackled. "Will you be available to run tomorrow? Like maybe you could take a break around ten-ish in the morning?"

He probably could take time off. He didn't need to spend every second at the office and getting out would be a great excuse to go to the shelter afterward. "I'm available."

"Good. I can meet you at the office."

"I'd like that." He crossed his ankles. "I'm looking forward to seeing you."

"In those shorty shorts," Kevin said. "I'll bet you're hot in yours."

"I'll bet you are, too."

"I try."

Kevin was opening up, and just thinking about that made Shaun smile. He liked Kevin's growing ease. "Text me when you're done."

"I will." Kevin sighed. "I don't know if you feel it, but I like where we're at. It's a good place."

"It is." He'd never been this happy before. "You're a great guy and I got lucky."

"You're silly, but you're a great guy, too," Kevin said. "Shit. Gotta go. I'm being paged. Talk to you later."

"You bet." He hung up and thought about Remy's question. Was he happy in Cedarwood?

Very, and things would only get better.

* * * *

Kevin woke Tuesday morning with his muscles still tense from the night before. *Damn.* He wished the tension in his body was from good sex, but no. Work sucked and he was still carrying the stress. He'd forgotten to text Shaun, which annoyed him, and he'd had to work the beer counter…again. Either the ballclub needed to hire more concessions staff, or something. He needed more personnel, because his people were stretched too thin and it was only two-thirds of the way through the season.

He needed help.

Sex wouldn't be bad, either.

He rubbed his forehead, then swatted the bed for Leo. The cat had curled up beside him — good for stress reduction, since he could pet Leo, but bad for having someone sleep over. Leo didn't like to share the bed.

He checked the clock as he petted Leo. At this rate, he had enough time to get himself hydrated and dressed before he'd told Shaun they'd meet up. If he didn't get moving, he'd end up being late. He poured a glass of water, and while he checked the messages on his work phone, he hydrated. His new personal phone would be in later that afternoon, but he'd have to wait until the ballgame concluded before he could pick it up.

Excitement filled his brain. He couldn't wait to see Shaun and run off some of his blossoming energy. That said, he should eat something or he'd run out of steam halfway through the run.

He grabbed a granola bar and plopped a scoop of Leo's dry food into his dish. Afterward, he read through his emails while he continued to drink his water. He couldn't recall being this happy and relaxed…ever. Unlike most men he knew, Shaun didn't need to be impressed — he liked Kevin, despite his awkwardness. Plus, they had things in common. The date, running, loving too much and too fast... He'd found a real partner in Shaun and they hadn't been a couple that long.

He paced the length of the living room and finished his granola bar. The protein should be coursing through his body by the time he headed out for the run.

His phone buzzed with a new email. He checked the sender's name.

Kyle.

Damn it.

Leo skittered across the floor and hopped onto the cat tree. He settled at the top and peered at Kevin.

"Sorry." Kevin opened the email. It could be something for work, but he rather doubted it.

K,

Heard you and Mr. Fallows are an item. You must really like him. Hope it works out.

K

Kevin frowned. The tone of the email was so unlike Kyle. He'd never been this positive. Sure, he could be turning over a new leaf, but Kyle liked his ways. He wondered what Kyle meant or if he'd even written it. He closed the email and shook his head. For all he knew, Kyle was just trying to psych him out.

He deleted the message and vowed not to let Kyle annoy him. This was the time to move forward.

He retrieved the muscle tape from the drawer. Once he cut pieces of the tape to affix to his calf muscles, he smoothed everything into place. The tension on his calf helped during the run to keep his muscle from getting too sore and kept the blood flowing better. He donned his running shoes, then grabbed his work phone, keys and wallet. With Shaun coming along, he didn't need to carry his ID and could keep that and his phone in the car.

Kevin petted Leo's head. "I'll be back later, then I have to work. Don't get angry with me. Either I work and provide kitty food or I don't and you go hungry."

Leo batted at him, then curled up on the cat tree.

"Whatever, brat." Kevin locked up and headed downstairs to his vehicle. Movement out of the corner of his eye caught his attention. He gazed across the lot and swore he saw Kyle's car, but that couldn't be. Kyle should be at work.

He ignored the strange car and slid behind the wheel of his own, then left the lot to head over to the newspaper offices. He listened to the radio. The pop music station wasn't his thing, but the songs buoyed his mood. His excitement increased. He couldn't wait to get running. He loved the fresh air in his lungs, the burn in his muscles and the feel of the asphalt and dirt under his feet. Running felt like he was making progress.

He parked next to Shaun in the newspaper lot and half expected to see Shaun stretched across his hood again. God, the vision of Shaun that way was so sexy and a great surprise. He replayed the memory of it over and over. Everyone wanted to know who'd been waiting for him. Nedra teased him, saying she was both jealous and thrilled for him.

Kevin entered the newspaper offices and strode up to Cara's desk in the foyer. She waved.

"Hi. I'm waiting on Shaun Fallows," he said. "I don't have an appointment."

"I'll bet not—you're dressed for a workout, not a business meeting." She tapped her tablet. "He's on his way. I hear you're his new squeeze."

"I am." He liked the way that sounded.

"You know, when he started here, I hoped he was straight. I mean, he's cute." Her eyes flashed. "Since he's not and you're just as cute, I'm glad he's with you."

"Thanks." He hadn't talked to Cara much, but he'd seen her around town and at the stadium a few times. She seemed nice enough.

"He should be right up." She folded her hands. "Think the team will get themselves back on track and start a winning streak? I thought they had a shot at the playoffs, but at this rate, they'll be lucky to finish at .500."

"They might." He wasn't good at discussing the team because he didn't pay any attention. He simply looked at the score. If they were winning, he wasn't terribly busy. If they were losing, then all hell broke loose at the concession stands. "They're trying."

"I hope so." She sighed. "We need something to cheer about in this town. It's so boring these days. Nothing's happening."

"I heard the Baker brothers are getting a street fair organized in conjunction with the 5k race. The ballclub is considering doing a satellite shop in town during the race and if there's a festival." He kept expecting a nudge to find a way to sell food at the presumed festivities. He knew nothing about food trucks and thought the town should showcase the restaurants before the stadium concessions.

"Now that's a good idea. People forget they can get merch for the team," she said. "We should have merch for the paper. Even if it's just stuff to give away."

"Tell your boss." Her idea wasn't bad, but might cost more money than Remy would want to pay. "I hear the paper is a sponsor of the race, so the name will be on those shirts."

"You're right." She grinned. "But I'm going to tell Mr. Nicholas. Who knows, we might have other shirts or something we can use for promotion." She nodded. "Here comes Shaun."

Shaun strolled down the corridor and his smile widened as he opened his arms. "Hi." He'd dressed in mid-thigh length shorts and a loose T-shirt.

"Hi." He hugged Shaun, not caring who saw them together. "Ready?"

"Very. It's been hectic this morning and I need a break." He kept his arm around Kevin, but spoke to Cara. "I told Remy I'll be back just after lunch. See you."

Kevin walked along with Shaun, not sure if he should tell Cara bye or not. "You're allowed to be away for that long?" Kevin asked. "I'm impressed. If I go over my allotted time, someone hunts me down."

"They might, but I'm not answering." Shaun stopped outside at the bench in front of the building. "I need to stretch, to run and to not think about how the fucking advertisements were screwed up between my final approval and the paper printing."

"Ouch." Kevin ran through his battery of stretches. If Shaun wanted to talk, he'd listen, but he wouldn't push him to divulge the details.

"It wouldn't have been so bad if so much hadn't gone haywire. The printer put page five in the lifestyle section twice, so that had to be re-run because, of course, we did the early edition run before it was checked. We started a longer run after it got caught, but I've had to scour the remaining pages to be sure they're not messed up. I already scoured them and now I'll end up doing it again. It's maddening."

"I bet." He didn't know there were multiple editions of the paper. "Is it finally sorted out?"

"For now." Shaun double-knotted his shoes, then sat on the concrete. "It wouldn't have been so bad, but I had to field phone calls from the baseball team reps."

Kevin frowned. "Why?"

"We decided to do a special mini-paper that features the team. It'll be at the stadium and free for everyone, but will include advertising for the services at the facility, spotlights on the team members and so forth. It was approved on our end and by the team, but I got static from their ad people. They seemed to think we're overstepping." He grabbed his toes as he stretched. "It's not overstepping if it's essentially free promo and eighty percent about the damn team."

"The promo department is touchy," Kevin said. "They get funny when I try to promote the food deals." He finished his stretches. "I don't know, but don't let it bother you. They love static and to be a pain in the ass. It's not personal."

"But we're helping them."

"I know." He bowed his head. Kyle ran the promo department with the team and probably wanted to piss Shaun off. "You're dealing with a somewhat unreasonable person. That's why he's giving you trouble — that and it's Kyle."

Shaun sat up. "Really? He's that petty?"

"Maybe more." Kevin tucked his car key into his zipped pocket and ensured he'd locked his vehicle. "I'm ready when you are. I forgot to bring my tunes, so I'm ready."

"I'm ready." Shaun stood. "And I'm tired of thinking about the paper. I need to get this frustration out."

"We could have sex," Kevin said. The words tumbled out before he could stop them, but he didn't regret it.

Shaun stared at him. His smile returned. "I would love that, but we don't have time."

At least he hadn't balked. "We'll put it on the list." He wouldn't mind a good masturbation session or oral sex right now, even if he did want to run. All three would be a great stress relief.

"Let's go before I change my mind and drag you into my office for a quickie." Shaun swatted Kevin's ass. "We'll discuss the terms of my surrender to you when we're done."

"Surrender?"

"Yes." Shaun inched closer. "The moment I give you my ass and let you do every naughty thing you want to do."

Kevin shivered. He liked the sound of that. "Shaun."

"I know. It's the wrong time." Shaun laughed. "Wednesday?"

"Yes." Kevin allowed himself to breathe. "Ready?" He tapped his watch, setting the timepiece and GPS. "Let's go."

Shaun darted off first, leaving Kevin in the dust.

"Brat." Kevin hurried to catch up to him, then fell into the steady cadence of Shaun's steps. He wasn't much of a talker when he ran. He preferred to focus on the run and how his body reacted. Chatting just got in the way.

"Do you have a distance you want to go?" Shaun asked. "I sort of have a course for five miles."

"Good," Kevin said and measured his breaths. "I'm following you." He didn't care where they ran as long as they got the miles in. He liked Shaun's pace — not too fast, but steady. As they continued along, perspiration sprouted on his body and his shirt stuck to his chest. He wanted to strip his shirt off, but hesitated. *Too soon?*

Shaun grabbed the hem of his own shirt and wrangled the garment over his head. He tucked part of the shirt into the waistband of his shorts and continued on.

Kevin nearly swallowed his tongue. He'd thought Shaun was sexy with his clothes in place, but sans shirt? *Holy hell.* Kevin held back a couple steps to admire Shaun's body. He spied a bit of ink on Shaun's shoulder blade. "You have a tattoo."

"I do."

Kevin caught up to him. "Did it hurt?"

"Falling from heaven because I'm an angel?" Shaun asked and laughed. "I'll tell you about my ink when we're done. It's not that exciting."

Oh, he wouldn't agree. He wanted to run his fingers over the tattoo and everywhere else on Shaun's body.

Shaun held up his hand. "That's two miles. If we turn back, we'll have four. If we go twice around the square, that'll add the extra mile."

"Do it." Kevin lost himself in the run, logging steps and fighting the urge to stare at Shaun. Nothing else mattered right now — just being with his man. He navigated around the town square twice, then kept up with Shaun as they ran back to the newspaper office. By the time they reached their destination, Kevin needed a water break. His muscles ached in a good way and he needed to catch his breath, but he'd loved every second of the run.

"You're not too bad." Shaun settled on the grass in front of the building and propped his feet on the back of the bench. "Gotta elevate."

"Recuperation is good." Kevin joined him on the ground and propped his legs on the bench. "I'm told we don't have to do this. If we simply recline in the grass, we're good."

"I read that, too, but we always did this after cross country events, so it's just part of my post-run activities." Shaun tucked one arm behind his head and rested his free hand on Kevin's belly. "But we used to do a lot of things back then that I wouldn't do now."

"Like?"

"Let stupid stuff bother me." Shaun tipped his head and grinned. "Like eat an entire pizza by myself." He shrugged. "Or let my dick run my life."

"We've all done that at one time or another." Kevin rested his hand on Shaun's and sighed. "I'm coming to realize there's no point in looking back unless you're learning from it. You know?"

"I do."

A shadow darkened over Kevin and he turned his attention to the invader. He shielded his eyes. "Remy?"

"Hi." Remy knelt on the bench. "I see two runners prepping for the race. Good. We need stout runners to represent the paper."

Shaun groaned. "I haven't asked him about being a participant on behalf of the paper."

Kevin propped himself up on his elbows. "Wait. What?"

"I'm supposed to ask you if you'd like to wear a *Tribune* shirt when you run." Shaun covered his face with both arms. "It's not required."

"No, but I'd appreciate it if you would," Remy said. "I'm pushing and I shouldn't, but this would be a great time to promote the paper and show we're involved in the community."

Kevin sighed. Shaun had said he'd signed him up for the race, but he wasn't sure if he could represent the paper. Kevin would probably be expected to wear something advertising the baseball team. Or, they might not care. "I'll consider it."

"That's the best I can ask for. Thanks." Remy left the bench. "You're going to the shelter, right?"

"It's next on the hit parade," Shaun said. "After lunch."

"Get a sandwich from the food truck and get moving." Remy walked away, leaving Kevin alone with Shaun.

"I'm sorry. He's determined and pushy sometimes." Shaun planted his feet on the ground and sat up. "He's been pestering me to ask you about the race."

"It's okay." Kevin folded his legs up, then stretched his back. "It might be a problem if I wear any promotion for anything, but I'll see." He didn't care what the team said. He wasn't actually part of the ballclub—he worked in the food service department. If the race wasn't sponsored by the team, then they didn't have a say.

"Don't hurt yourself finding out. Remy will live and I just want you to be there."

"I know." Kevin sat up. "I need to head out soon. The game is at two-thirty and we start set-up at one. It's tedious, but it's a living."

"You need to help set up? You can't just watch? You're management."

"But when we're short of workers, I have to jump in."

"You did the last time."

"And I'll keep doing it until they hire more people."

"You can't get more help?" Shaun asked.

"I'd love to, but they won't advertise." Kevin stood. "What are you doing at the shelter? A story?" He wanted to change the subject and stop discussing the team.

"I'm doing a feature on the animals, a pet of the week thing," Shaun said. "I'll get an interview with Stone to start, then photograph some of the animals. The idea is to get them homes."

"Nice." He liked the idea of Shaun branching out. "Stone's a good guy. He'd keep every animal at his farm if it was possible. I've considered going up to the shelter and getting a companion for Leo. Maybe one of your features will be the one we're looking for."

"Could be." Shaun tipped his head. "Wait. Stone has a farm?"

"And a donkey. Ask him."

"I'm not shocked." Shaun stood. He kissed Kevin and curled his fingers under Kevin's chin. "It's going to be forever when I see you again."

"It's not that long to wat." Kevin nuzzled Shaun's cheek. "Plus, it gives us time to explore each other."

"Yes." He brushed his lips over Kevin's. "I had a good run because you were with me. We'll have to find time tomorrow, too."

"We will." Kevin remained close for another moment. He'd ache until he got to see Shaun again, but it only made him like Shaun more. "I'll try to text you tonight."

"Tell Leo I said hi." Shaun let go. "I miss the furball."

"He's addicting." Kevin kissed him once more, then gathered himself. "Talk to you later?"

"You bet." Shaun winked. "You're sexy when you sweat."

"So are you." He paused. "And I want to know about that ink. It's hot."

"I'll tell you tomorrow." Shaun wriggled his eyebrow. "Go before you're late."

Kevin hurried to his car. He slid behind the wheel and checked he had everything—phone, keys, wallet. *Phone display silent. Good, no missed calls.* He waved to Shaun, then drove home. When he checked his mailbox, his new phone had arrived.

He carried the mail and box up to his apartment. While the phone charged enough to use it, Kevin showered. By the time he finished, the device had already synced up with the information from the ruined one.

Kevin dressed and ate his lunch, then fiddled with the new device. According to his personal email, he had fourteen new messages. He also had a slew of missed texts and five calls. The missed calls were expected since he hadn't told most people his phone was down. At least three of the texts were from Shaun and one call was from Kyle.

What does Kyle want?

He checked the missed calls. A part of him felt guilt about missing the texts and calls, but he hadn't received the texts until now and hadn't known anyone had called him. That, and he'd worked things out with Shaun.

Leo hopped onto the table and batted at Kevin's hand. Kevin kept fiddling with his phone, but also scratched Leo's head. He appreciated Leo's ability to relax him. The cat seemed to know when he needed soothing.

He opened his emails and thanked God nothing was important—mostly messages from Kyle about his exploits clubbing. He should delete Kyle's number and email address. Could block him, too. Kyle was nothing but a bad influence.

Kevin deleted the emails, then set the wallpaper image. He should get a photo with Shaun to show everyone. He texted Shaun.

New phone up and running. Won't dunk it. Promise. Had a good run today, too. You're a fun partner. You pushed me.

He hit Send, then finished his lunch. He placed the dishes in the dishwasher, then left a single treat square in Leo's dish.

"Be good. I need to go to work. Don't knock stuff over." He rubbed Leo's head, then left the cat to eat. He put on his shoes, grabbed his phones and wallet, then keys and locked up.

He headed down to his car. The run with Shaun had refreshed him. He could handle anything today. Let the stress come. He was ready. He drove to the stadium. Once he headed into the building, he jumped right into the thick of setting up. Enough workers had shown up, giving him the chance to catch up on ordering stock for the upcoming games.

Nedra cornered him in the kitchen. "Hi, you."

"Hi." Kevin inputted the next set of numbers, then stretched. "What can I do for you?"

"Me? Nothing. Kyle? Face him. I don't know what he needs you for, but he's being a pain in my ass. He's promo and we're concessions, but he's lurking," she said. "He has no standing with us, not that he cares."

"But if I can convince him to go along with it, we'll get new banners and can advertise our food better." Kevin saved the order and darkened the tablet screen. "Where is he?" He might as well get this over with.

"Your office."

He snorted. He had an office, but almost never used it. Instead, he kept a locker like the rest of his staff. The office was more of a breakroom for anyone who wanted to use it and had once been the place he met with Kyle for blowjobs. If Kyle wanted head, he could go somewhere else. "I'll head over there."

"Good luck. He seems pissed."

"When is he not?" Kevin left the stock room and navigated around the building to his office. With the door open, he saw Kyle sitting on top of his desk. Kevin stopped in the doorway. "Kyle. You requested me?"

"I did." Kyle remained on the desk. "Close the door."

Back in the day, that had been the code phrase for head. "I'll keep it open. What do you want?"

"A conversation with you. Close the door." Kyle pointed at Kevin. "Do it."

"No."

"Kevin." Kyle groaned and slouched on the desk. "Don't be like this."

"You need to stop. What we had was in the past and it's going to stay there. We work at the same place — that's it. We were together and we split. Accept it. Stop calling me about silly things and don't email me. You don't need me." His heart hammered. He'd never stood up for himself like this and he liked the rush of adrenaline.

"You don't know that." Kyle left the desk. "What do you see in Shaun? What's he got that I don't? Huh? The cat? Does he like Shaun or has he tried to claw his eyes out?"

"Shaun and Leo get along." Kevin folded his arms. "Next issue."

"Leo is a cat."

"And part of the family." Kyle would never understand. To him, animals were nothing more and never would be.

"You give that rotten cat so much control," Kyle said. "A cat can adjust." He crossed the room and yanked Kevin into the space, then shut the door. "Now forget about them, because I need you."

Kevin ducked out of Kyle's range. "No."

"No? We were tight and you love me."

Kevin gritted his teeth. "I did, but you didn't love me in return. I can't do this with you. I can't let myself get hurt again. I'm tired."

"Kevin."

"The biggest thing is that I'm with someone and I'm not cheating on him with you." He darted around Kyle and left the office. He hated that he'd let Kyle get under his skin. So he'd given the cat a lot of control. The cat was still part of his family. But more than that, he'd bestowed too much power on Kyle. He'd allowed Kyle and his manipulations to steamroll him. *Christ.* Kyle thought he could come back at any time and his mood swings didn't matter. *Bullshit.*

Kevin headed out to the concessions area and Nedra waved at him.

"Help," she said. "I can't keep up." She loaded racks of buns onto the rolling cart. "We're short-handed again."

He glanced at the score. The game was only in the second inning, but the team was down by four. *Shit.* Kevin sighed. Unless he jumped in to help and spoke up to the powers that be, nothing would get fixed.

Kevin assumed one of the positions at the counter and took orders. He helped patrons, but considered what he wanted to do to change the staff problems. If the team kept losing, there was a good chance the crowds would dwindle. Unfortunately, a losing streak meant no one wanted to be there. He couldn't justify having more people to help with concessions if the crowds weren't there to eat the food.

He rolled his shoulders. At least he had a job. He'd worry about the staffing issues later.

Chapter Five

Shaun rolled away from his desk and checked the layout on the board on the wall. He needed to keep his mind off Kevin. He'd watched the baseball score online the day before and winced at the crushing loss. The last time the team had played so poorly, Kevin had been worked hard. He hadn't heard from his boyfriend the night before, and while it annoyed him, he understood.

He couldn't wait for their lunch date, but had no details, so had no idea when Kevin might turn up.

Cara stood in his doorway. "Hi. I'm heading out for lunch. Want to come along?"

"I'm good here, thanks."

"You look sad." She leaned on the doorframe and folded her arms. "Are you okay?"

"I'm okay." He sagged in his chair. "I'm lovesick, that's what I am. Isn't that terrible?"

"Lovesick? Over Kevin?"

"Yeah."

"It's not terrible." She shrugged. "You've got a new relationship. You want to be with him—which is normal."

"He's always busy." He sounded whiny, but he didn't care. He needed to hit the release valve and let some of it out. "I'm sorry, but it's just that I thought I loved Jonah and it fizzled, but how I felt about him was never like this. Because this is new?"

"I don't know."

"I've never been in this deep and I don't know what to do."

"You're exclusive, right? He's not seeing anyone else, I assume, so don't sweat it." She stood tall. "It sure seems like you're holding on too tight and don't have to, but I get it. Remember, he's yours, so enjoy yourself. Just because he doesn't call you or whatever doesn't mean he doesn't care. Have faith in him and in yourself."

"You don't think it's my biological clock or anything?"

She snorted. "Probably. You're cruising toward middle age and afraid you'll end up alone. I get that because I feel the same way, but it's not necessarily our fate. You've got a good man and I'll find mine. Don't let your insecurities get the better of you."

She had a point. His issues all boiled down to insecurities. He'd been hurt before and feared he would be again. It seemed like his worry was getting the better of him and threatening to destroy his faith. It could destroy his relationship with Kevin, too.

"It's cool that you're concerned. You should be. Life is crazy, but give yourself a chance," she said.

He nodded. "Thanks." She'd given him a ton to think about.

"So, do you want to come along, now that you've unloaded? Ned, Francis, Gail, Serena and I are heading to the Diner." She rapped her knuckles on the doorframe. "Hmm?"

"I'm going to stay here and cool my heels. Thanks," Shaun said. "How about another time? Kevin should be by any minute now."

"Well, that's a better offer." She smiled. "I'll check on you later." She left him alone with his thoughts.

Shaun sighed and thought back to his time with Jonah. Things had fallen apart because he and Jonah had wanted different things. He wanted to be married and settle down. Jonah had wanted to roam. Instead of listening to Jonah's cues, Shaun had blundered ahead with his plans and ended up hurt. Now he'd blown forward and jumped in deep with Kevin, mentioning marriage. Cara was right. He needed to slow down. The good feelings concerning Kevin buoyed him and he saw the future with Kevin. Why would he want to destroy things when they were just getting started?

A knock on the door yanked him from his thoughts. "Are you home?"

"Kevin." He met Kevin's gaze. His man was there, dressed in board shorts, a T-shirt and running shoes. So casual, but he also looked happy.

"In the flesh." Kevin held a bag and grinned. "I brought food."

"Thanks." Shaun moved the clutter from his desk. "Come in."

"I wanted to text you last night, but we got creamed and food service got slammed." Kevin ventured into the office and placed the bag on the desk. "Then I got the nerve up to mention we needed help, but I got my ass handed to me by my boss because there isn't money coming in to pay for more people."

"Kevin." Damn. He wished he could've saved Kevin the headache.

"I know. I shouldn't have aimed above my station at this time, but we were so overwhelmed and I got tired of it." Kevin sat across from him. "I brought gyros. The gyro truck has awesome food."

"Smells delicious." He withdrew a bottle of hand sanitizer out of his desk. "Have some." He cleaned his hands. "I haven't had a chance to visit most of the food trucks. The taco one is good."

"Agreed." Kevin used the sanitizer. "Anyway, I asked for help and got reamed and as a result, I lost two of the smaller concession counters. It condenses the workforce, so it gives us better numbers, but sucks because we'll probably lose money."

"Because the team is on a skid?" Shaun opened the foil around his gyro. The scent swirled around him. His mouth watered. "You know what? I don't care about work. I'm glad you're here. I missed you."

"I missed you, too. I wish we could've had a run this morning, but we'll get a schedule going." Kevin withdrew two bottles of water. "I wanted lemonade, but they'd run out."

"Oh well." Shaun groaned as he bit into his gyro. "This is so good." He hadn't realized how hungry he was until now and devoured the sandwich. The flavors melted on his tongue. He wanted to continue the conversation, but the gyro was too delicious.

Kevin stopped eating long enough to take a draw from his water. "I love the gyros, but I can't eat them often or I'd have to run all the time." He laughed. "I love the fries, too. They have a funny coating on them that's so good, but I'm so tired of fries. I'm surrounded by them."

"Do you ever get tired of concessions food?" Shaun asked. "I'd get sick of it after a while."

"It goes in spurts. I'm not wild about hot dogs because I've had to cook them almost every day I've been at the stadium, but I liked when I worked at Jack's Hot Dog Shop," Kevin said. "It was frantic and claustrophobic at times, but fun."

"Jack mentioned you worked for him. He was in buying advertising space for the shop." Shaun finished his gyro. "You're right. This is addictive."

"I know," Kevin said. "So tell me about that ink."

Shaun's cheeks heated. He'd forgotten about his tattoo. "Eat and I'll tell you." He balled up his foil. "When I was seventeen, I thought I needed to look tough. I thought if I had a tattoo, then I'd be respected. It wasn't the case, though. So I went to my mother and begged for permission to get inked. She said no and I had to wait. When I went to college, I had a job working at the desk in my dorm. I saved my pennies until I had enough to pay for the tattoo. My friend, Shelby, had a tattoo shop. I went to him for what was supposed to be a cross, but ended up being a cross and my initials — SMF." He shrugged. "I forget it's there. Once it healed over, it was no big deal."

"It's sexy." Kevin finished his gyro, then downed more of his water. "I'm too chicken to get inked." He shivered. "I'm not wild about needles, though. I give blood, but I have to look away when they jab me. Silly, isn't it? I'm a grown man who doesn't like needles. I like the way tattoos look on others, though."

"Ever want to get pierced?"

"I never thought about it."

"You'd be hot with your nipples pierced, but I'm not pushing."

"I never thought about it." Kevin crinkled his nose. "It sounds painful."

"Probably." He'd never considered it himself, but liked the look. "I dated a guy who had them. I didn't ask him if it hurt." He pressed his lips together. He shouldn't have brought up a former boyfriend.

"It might," Kevin said. "Do you regret your ink or are you proud?"

"I'm not regretful most of the time. It was an experience and I learned, so I guess it was worth the trouble." He collected the trash. "I realized I'm not the kind of guy who wants to be covered in tattoos." The temporary pain of being inked wasn't high on his list of things to do again. Besides, he had no idea what else he'd get.

"It's a commitment."

"True." Shaun sighed and settled in his seat. "I'm done in roughly an hour." He'd like to be done right now. He'd rather spend the rest of the afternoon with Kevin than fiddle with copy and minute changes. The pet shelter story wouldn't be hard, but he'd still rather be with Kevin.

"Come over. Leo wants to see you." Kevin's eyes flashed. "Yeah?"

"Do you want to see me?" He wasn't sure why he'd asked that. Kevin wouldn't invite him over if it wasn't real.

"Always." Kevin stood. "I'm off tonight and I'm sure we can find something to do. A movie, or TV show."

"Yes." He wanted to leave right now. He'd finish the pet feature in seconds if he could. "I'll sort out dinner."

"Deal. I need to run a couple errands, but I'll meet you at my place when you're done." Kevin tossed his garbage into the can. "It's going to be a great day."

He agreed. "Kevin?" He wasn't ready for Kevin to leave. They had such chemistry and he craved Kevin's attention.

"Yeah?" Kevin wiped his hands on a napkin. "What's up?"

"Nothing." Shaun wasn't sure what he wanted to say because his thoughts were a jumble. "I'll text you when I'm on my way." He left his seat and rounded his desk. "And right now, I'll walk you out."

"I'm not helpless. I know how I got here." Kevin held Shaun's hand. "But it's nice to be escorted."

"Accompanied." He bumped shoulders with Kevin. "You make me happy." He walked them out into the sunshine. "Things are falling into place."

Kevin frowned. "They are?"

"I wanted to start over in Cedarwood. Find myself, put down roots and find happiness," Shaun said. "I'm well on my way because I know what I want from my life and I've got a purpose—to write stories for the paper, do the advertising and be part of the community. My roots are starting to grow and I'm in a good place because I have you." He kissed Kevin. "See? Life is how it's supposed to be."

"Yes, it is."

Shaun's phone buzzed in his pocket. He'd almost forgotten he'd tucked the device away. "Sorry." He checked the name of the caller. "It's Remy and I should take it."

"Go ahead. I'll see you tonight, so it's not like you're bothering me." Kevin kissed him. "Deal with that, but don't goof around. I hate watching movies alone."

"You have Leo."

"He sits on my chest and obscures the view."

"That might be a problem." Shaun swiped to answer the call. "See you." He turned his attention to the phone. "Remy."

"Finally," Remy said. "I see you in the parking lot. Hurry up."

"Ouch." He waved to Kevin as he backed out of his spot. He kept waving until Kevin drove out of sight. Once his boyfriend was gone, Shaun walked into the building.

Remy stood in the foyer. "Sorry I had to call, but you weren't in your office. Where is everyone? Did I call a holiday and forget about it?"

"They went to lunch," Shaun said. "I thought you knew." What the staff did wasn't his business.

"Nope." Remy tucked his phone into his breast pocket. "The feature?"

"I'm polishing. It should be on your desk within the hour."

"Good," Remy said. "Get it done and you're good for the day. I like the photo you chose. The pup is cute."

"Cara liked it, too. She seemed interested in him." The mixed breed dog had adorable floppy ears and would make anyone a good pet. The little thing reminded Shaun of a mini Great Dane.

"She could use a dog." Remy nodded. "Get the story done. Go. I don't want to wait all day."

"Yes, sir." Shaun strolled into the office. Getting used to Remy's quirks took time, but he seemed to understand him better. Remy wanted stuff done now and had a short attention span. *Oh well.* Remy knew how to steer the paper in the right direction and Shaun didn't mind. He preferred to have deadlines and tasks.

Too much wiggle room got him into trouble because he tended to overanalyze and take extra time.

He settled behind his desk and opened his laptop. In moments, he got to work. The story didn't need much polish. It was straightforward and sleek. He added a couple of extra sentences, then sat back for a final read-through. If he fiddled with it any longer, he'd screw the story up. Instead, he sent the photo and article straight to Remy's email.

"Done," Shaun murmured. He rolled away from his desk and stretched. The weight of getting the story done was off his shoulders. He could relax tonight and enjoy his time with Kevin.

He logged out of his laptop and shut the computer down. After he packed up his things, he stopped by Remy's office. "I sent it through."

"Got it." Remy waved without looking up from his laptop. "You're off?"

"To see Kevin, yes."

"Have fun." Remy never switched his focus from the computer screen, like Shaun wasn't there.

Shaun should've been insulted, but he wasn't—no point. He sighed and returned to his office long enough to ensure he had everything, then switched off the lights and locked up. He headed out to his car. In just a little while, he'd be with Kevin.

He settled behind the wheel and plugged his phone into the charger. As he backed out of the spot, his phone rang and Cheryl's name came on the display screen. He tapped the button on the steering wheel to answer the call hands-free. "Hi."

"You're a hard man to reach," Cheryl said. "Where have you been?"

"How many times have you tried to call?" He navigated through town to the grocery store. "I haven't been MIA."

"I tried once, but I'm used to you just being there," she said. "Where have you been?"

"With Kevin and at work. It's been hectic. Between the proofs not being right and other stuff, I haven't had time to breathe."

"Kevin? You're still together?"

"I am, and he's great."

"When do I get to meet him?"

"Soon." He wanted to show off his boyfriend to everyone.

"Tell me about him," she said. "Not the 'he's sweet' bullshit. What do you know about him? This is happening fast. What is his favorite color? Cat's name? Is he allergic to shellfish? Come on. You don't know anything."

He pulled into the lot and parked, then disconnected his phone. He pressed the device to his ear. "He has a cat, so he's not allergic. The cat's name is Leo and he's a little choosy, but I like him. Besides, he's a cat. He's going to be a snot. As for shellfish, I haven't asked, but I will. I don't know his favorite color or even his birthday, but I will." He groaned. "We haven't slept together yet. The hottest thing we've done has been a five-mile run and a hot kiss at his apartment. I'm taking it slow, so I don't mess this up."

"I want to be mad at you, but I can't. You're being good, which is all I can ask." She sighed. "Just keep your head on. I know how you dive in deep, then flame out."

"I know," he said. "I need to go. I'm cooking for him tonight and I need to get stuff."

"Cooking for him?" She laughed. "You really are in over your head. You don't cook for anyone."

"It's not my idea of fun, but I want to do this." He tucked his wallet into his back pocket. "Anyway, I'll call you in a day or two. Okay? Love ya," he said. "Thanks for checking on me."

"Love you."

He hung up, then headed into the grocery store. He wasn't sure what to make. It probably didn't matter what he cooked, because he had plenty of time. Hell, they had all night. He wandered the aisles, seeking inspiration. None came to mind. He walked past the meat counter and spied the prepared meatballs and chicken dishes. A thought came to mind—he could make chicken with mozzarella and spaghetti. He picked up a package of chicken breasts, some fresh mozzarella cheese, pasta and a jar of sauce. Would Kevin like bread? The carbs might help with their run the next day. He should grab some.

He stopped at the frozen food section and picked out breadsticks.

"Shaun?" Jack strode up to him. "It's Jack. I bought an ad in the paper. It's nice to see you."

"Sure, I remember. Hi, Jack. How are you?" He had his arms full of stuff or he would've offered his hand. "How's sales?"

"Good."

"I'm glad to hear it. Your ad should be running now," Shaun said. "I like how it turned out."

"I saw it and it looks great. I may offer a coupon next time. Can I do that?" Jack asked.

"Sure can. Email me and we'll get it set up when you're ready." He jiggled the things in his arms. "Sorry."

"No worries," Jack said. "Got plans for tonight?"

"I'm cooking for Kevin tonight." He nodded to his purchases and hoped he didn't drop anything. "I hope it turns out okay."

"Looks like you have a good start." Jack tipped his ballcap. "I'll let you go. Have a great night and thanks for the advice. I'll be in touch."

"Good deal and good afternoon." Shaun headed to the register and paid, then left the store. He drove the short distance to Kevin's apartment. Halfway there, a though occurred to him — he should've bought wine or something. *Shit.*

Oh well. A forgotten bottle of wine wasn't going to ruin his evening. Nothing could. He was about to see Kevin and have a good time.

He deserved nothing less.

* * * *

Kevin cleaned the apartment and tried to ensure the place looked spotless. He doubted Shaun cared if his space was messy, but he refused to have a disaster. He didn't want a tumbleweed of cat hair on the carpet, cat toys on the floor or dirty dishes in the sink. He had to have this perfect.

Leo strutted across the coffee table and bopped the unlit candles onto the floor.

"Thanks." Kevin picked up the tea lights. *So much for setting the mood.* He placed the candles on the side table, then paced the length of the room. He should make sure he looked okay. He'd never thought he was handsome, but he was passable. Part of him knew he had Shaun's affection, but the niggling doubts came back. They always did. God, he had to stop being negative and worrying. Shaun wasn't Kyle and probably never would be.

He checked his outfit and fixed his hair. He'd paired a clean pair of khaki shorts with a different T-shirt. Should he wear socks? His slippers? Did it matter?

He groaned, then walked away from the mirror. Staring at himself wasn't going to help.

Where was Shaun? He sat on the couch and petted Leo. He hadn't been this worried with Kyle. Then again, with Kyle, he'd worried about how Kyle would react and if he'd even show up. With Shaun, he couldn't contain his excitement. He had to embrace the positivity. Shaun was the man he needed.

Leo sat on Kevin's lap and cleaned his paw, then licked his side.

"You don't care about any of this, do you?" He petted the cat. "What do you think of Shaun? Do you like him?"

Leo stopped bathing and stared at him. He didn't blink, just stared.

"I like him, Leo. I like him and I want this to work. He makes me laugh and I feel comfortable. I want to climb all over him, too. I got a hint of what he's packing and it's all I can do to keep myself from exploring. My God, and he seems to really like me. It's not fake, it's not forced... Leo...I might be in love."

His breath caught in his throat. He'd thought he loved Kyle, but realized it was only lust. The connection might have had a bit to do with punishment, too. He didn't feel like he deserved to be loved by a nice guy and had to settle for guys like Kyle. He knew damn well Kyle wasn't good for him. He'd known since they'd moved in together and Kyle had tossed most of Kevin's clothing because it wasn't designer label.

Shaun wasn't like that.

The door buzzer infiltrated his thoughts and Leo scrambled out of sight. Kevin jumped up from the couch. He checked his phone. One text from Shaun.

At the door. Can use help. Arms full.

Shit. He grabbed his keys and stuffed his feet into his boat shoes, then hurried to the ground floor. Shaun stood just outside the main door with two bags in his arms. He grinned.

Kevin opened the door. "Hi. Let me help you." He took one of the bags. "Are you feeding a mob?"

"No." Shaun laughed. "I overthought this, though."

"What are you making?" He opened the second door, allowing Shaun into the building.

"Baked chicken and pasta." Shaun waited for Kevin and ascended the stairs alongside him. "I got sidetracked by my friend and talked with Jack at the grocery store."

"Jack? Hot Dog Jack?"

"The one and only."

Kevin opened his apartment door. "How is he?"

"Good." Shaun carried his bag to the kitchen, then left the sack on the counter before he kicked out of his shoes by the door. "He wants to run a coupon."

Kevin placed his bag on the counter. "Cool." He didn't want to discuss Jack or coupons. "What can I help you do?"

"Right now, kiss me." Shaun threaded his arms around Kevin. "You're enough."

"Am I?" Kevin kissed him. "You look tired. Let me help you tonight."

"I appreciate it." Shaun held him. "Give me a minute. This is what I need most."

Kevin snuggled in Shaun's arms. He liked the way Shaun smelled and how he and Shaun truly fit together. He nuzzled Shaun's throat.

Shaun stroked Kevin's back. "When I'm right here, everything in the world is balanced."

"Because it is." Kevin smoothed his palm over the back of Shaun's neck. "I don't know how we didn't run into each other earlier, but I'm glad I met you."

Shaun squeezed Kevin's ass. "My thoughts exactly."

"We should get dinner going before Leo gets into it," Kevin said. "I see him peeking around the corner. He'll be digging in those bags in no time. He's nosy."

"I'll bet." Shaun disengaged from him. "Let's get this to the kitchen and cook the chicken. Want to turn on the oven?" He washed his hands, then dried them on the towel.

"Sure." Kevin followed suit, then emptied one of the bags on the counter. "Ooh, you got fresh mozzarella cheese. I think I'm in love."

"I prefer fresh over the blocky chunks that you're not sure how long have been there." Shaun opened the package of chicken. "I thought about it after I purchased the bundle. I remember asking you if you were allergic, but things can happen or can be forgotten in the rush. I should've asked again before I went shopping."

Kevin withdrew a skillet from the cupboard. "Here. You're going to need that to brown the chicken." He grabbed the spray. "This is what I use to keep it from sticking to the pan."

"Thanks. Will you turn the oven to three-seventy-five, please? Oh, and I need a knife to clean the chicken." Shaun blushed. "I guess I'm pushy and didn't plan this well, did I?"

Kevin located the paring knife and cutting board. "It's okay. You're getting more cooking done in here than I tend to do. Want me to start the water for the spaghetti?"

"Sure." Shaun sprayed the pan and set it on the burner, then focused on the chicken.

While Shaun worked on the main course, Kevin added water and salt to a saucepan, then dribbled a bit of oil into the water.

"I'll turn this one once you get the chicken into the skillet." Kevin rested his hip against the counter. "As for allergic to lactose, I'm not."

"Good." Shaun finished cleaning the chicken, then washed his hands and turned on the burner. "My friend Cheryl called me. We were apartment mates in college. Us and three other people. Made the rent better and we had our own little squad that way. She studied finance and works at a bank, and I went toward advertising. All these years later, we still check on each other every so often. She called while I was on my way over here to see what I was doing. I told her...you. Why don't you turn the water on? Do you have tongs to turn the chicken?"

"Here." He grabbed the tongs and turned on the burner. "How is she?" He had no idea who this Cheryl was, but she sounded nice and Shaun hadn't made a big deal about him mentioning the L world.

"She's good. She divorced her husband about five years ago and never quite got her groove back. I think she's waiting for the right guy to come along." Shaun shrugged. "Took me this long to find you, so I doubt I'm going to be much help to her. But she called." He turned the chicken over. "She wanted to know about you."

"And you told her?" He retrieved the pasta tool from the drawer. "My vital stats?"

"Sort of." Shaun moved the chicken around in the pan. "She asked a bunch of questions I can't answer."

"Like?"

"Your favorite color, your birthday…middle name. Stuff like that." Shaun turned the chicken pieces over again. "She got after me for not knowing."

"She's just concerned." Kevin opened the box of pasta. He didn't blame her for wanting the information, since she wanted to make sure he was happy and safe. "It's the sign of a good friend."

"She'd like hearing that—or she'd call you a sweet-talker."

Kevin moved the pasta around in the pot. "My middle name is Reece. It was my mother's maiden name and she liked it. My favorite color is pink. I love how it looks so delicate and pretty, but can be garish, too. I'll take any color over black—my work clothes are black and it's so boring."

"Makes sense. Plus, you end up with a huge headache when you're at work."

"I do," Kevin said. He checked the time on the pasta and calculated how much time it had left to cook. "My birthday is February twenty-fifth." He met Shaun's gaze. "What about you?"

"Shaun Michael Fallows. I was born on April nineteenth. I don't have a favorite color, though." He grinned. The circles under his eyes seemed to fade. "I love classical music and listen to Mozart to settle my mind when I'm stressed."

Kevin stirred the pasta. "I don't think I could pick out a piece by Mozart if I tried."

"You know more than you realize." Shaun turned the chicken over again. "Do you have a cheese slicer?"

"It's better if you use a knife." Kevin abandoned the pasta and withdrew another knife from the block. "Like this." He cut pieces from the chunk of cheese. "It'll be so gooey and delicious."

"I know." Shaun kissed his cheek. "This is so nice. I've never had anyone want to cook with me."

"You've been with the wrong people." Kevin rubbed Shaun's back, then pressed his mouth to the soft spot where his neck connected to his shoulder.

Shaun sliced the cheese. "We'll need a pan to put this in the oven so we can melt the cheese."

"Done." Kevin produced the pan and sprayed it. "Go for it."

Shaun grinned. "Should be about time to drain the pasta."

"On it." Kevin turned off the burner, then placed the colander in the sink. "Watch out." He carried the pot to the sink and drained the water. Steam billowed. "Whew."

"While this melts, add the sauce and put the pot on the remaining heat." Shaun pushed the pan into the oven. "Won't be long now."

"Nope." Kevin did as told and mixed the pasta and sauce. "You must be a good influence. I'm never this slick in the kitchen. I make more of a mess than food actually cooked."

"It happens," Shaun said. "I didn't bring wine, so we'll need something else to drink."

"Water works." Kevin poured two glasses of water, then added a bit of food to Leo's bowl. He retrieved two plates, napkins and silverware. "We can eat at the coffee table again. It's sort of our spot."

"It is."

Kevin left Shaun in the kitchen and set the coffee table. He arranged the silver and napkins, then carried out the water glasses.

"Potholder?" Shaun opened the oven a crack. "It's melted."

Kevin stole a piece of cheese and popped it into his mouth. The creamy goodness slid over his tongue and down his throat. He offered the potholder to Shaun.

"Thank you." Shaun withdrew the pan from the oven and turned it off. "This is ready."

"Smells fantastic."

"I should've seasoned the chicken more." Shaun frowned. "I didn't add anything beyond salt and pepper."

"You've got the pasta and cheese. It'll be fine." Kevin plated the pasta and arranged the chicken on top. "Here." He hand shredded cheese on top of each piece of chicken.

"Nice touch." Shaun carried his plate to the coffee table.

Kevin followed, then turned on the music. "I know it's not only Mozart, but this channel has some pretty dinner music."

Shaun beamed. "You remembered?"

"I listened to you." Kevin sat beside him on the floor and leaned on the sofa. "If this tastes half as good as it smells, then it'll be delish."

"I hope so." Shaun sighed. "This is how I want to end my day. Good food, great environment, a cat staring at us while we eat, and you." He kissed Kevin's cheek. "Thanks for bringing me lunch, but does he always stare at you while you eat?"

"Always. Usually he paws at me, too." He'd gotten so used to the cat staring at him that he didn't notice. "As for lunch, you looked like you needed a break." Kevin ate his dinner. The mozzarella melted in his mouth. The chicken was tender and juicy. "This is good."

Shaun smiled. "I didn't burn it, so there's that."

"It's wonderful." Kevin ate in relative silence and stole glances at Shaun. Even Leo didn't interrupt dinner. He stared at them, but didn't try to walk on the table. Kevin had to agree with Shaun—this was the best way to end his day. He had his boyfriend beside him, the cat and the perfect atmosphere.

How can one man get so lucky?

Chapter Six

After dinner, Shaun helped clean up and wash the dishes. He liked the companionship he'd built with Kevin. They were a team already, pleasant and easy. Sure, he and Kevin would probably fight—he'd never asked Kevin about his political views or if he liked rave music—but did those things matter? They could agree to disagree. He wasn't one for rave music, but so what if Kevin did? They didn't have to love every single thing together. He wanted Kevin to have his own things and for them to have a difference of opinion.

"Do you see your folks often?" Kevin asked. He draped the soggy dishtowel over the oven handle. "I don't get to see mine much. Mom's still a nurse and working. Dad retired from the glass factory and putters in his garage."

"I call my mom every month, but not as much as I'd like. My parents split and I don't have any contact with my dad since he remarried." Shaun shrugged. He didn't like his father's wife, but she was only a few years older than Shaun. He couldn't see how she and his father had much in common.

"I'm sorry to hear that." Kevin wandered out to the sofa. "Want to watch a movie?"

"Got any suggestions? I'm game." Shaun sat beside him.

"How about an old Cary Grant flick?" Kevin opened his laptop and tapped the internet icon. He placed the device on the coffee table.

"Sure." There was so much he didn't know about Kevin, but a ton he did know. Kevin was a romantic, a sweet guy, caring and had a big heart.

Leo strolled into the room and jumped into Kevin's lap. "And someone wants attention."

"He's fine." Shaun scratched Leo behind the ears. "We have to share, though."

Leo blinked and didn't otherwise move.

"He's settled in." Kevin pointed to the laptop. "If you tap Start and join me, he'll snuggle up on the couch with us."

"I heard he's a tough customer, but he seems to like me — okay, he tolerates me." Shaun tapped the icon and started the movie, then stretched out on his side lengthwise on the sofa.

Kevin lay with him, his back to Shaun's belly. Leo climbed on top of Kevin's side, resting on his hip.

Shaun draped his arm around Kevin. He liked the idea of them being one happy family. Sure, they could use a bigger place with a yard, but they'd get there. This moment was the best. He paid little attention to the movie. Cary Grant was dashing, but Kevin was better.

Leo hopped off Kevin and disappeared into the other room. Shaun stretched. "How long until he returns?" Shaun asked. "Or did I offend him?"

"Potty break." Kevin rolled onto his back. "Let me guess. Your friend thinks we're moving too fast. Is that the gist of her call? It's been bugging me all through dinner and the movie. I hate letting people down."

"She said that, but her beef is with me. I tend to lead with my heart, not my head." He smoothed the wrinkles in Kevin's shirt. "Why would it bother you? Don't let her mess with you."

"It got me to thinking about what Nedra said. She and I work together and she said the same thing. She likes you, but wants me to be careful after Kyle." Kevin laced his fingers with Shaun's, then tugged him on top. "I don't think it's been that fast."

"No?" He agreed, but Kevin had caught him off-guard with his line of discussion.

"I think we need to rev it up."

"You do?" Shaun grinded on Kevin. Blood rushed to his dick and his entire being sizzled. He'd bet the sparks were visible. "What do you want to do?"

Kevin's eyes flashed. "You, then you do me."

"Yes." He kissed Kevin and cupped his jaw in his hand as he straddled Kevin's legs. He rubbed his groin on Kevin's. His need reached a fever pitch in seconds. He'd waited so long for this moment.

Kevin opened to him and sucked on Shaun's tongue. Shaun groaned. His boyfriend tasted good. Hot and decadent. He bumped noses with him a few times and couldn't get enough. He needed to be closer to Kevin. The scent of him curled around Shaun's nose.

Kevin broke the kiss. "Fuck me."

"Soon." He inched down Kevin's body until he settled between his legs. "Shirt. Off."

Kevin sat up long enough to remove the garment. Shaun gazed at his prize. A tad thin and only a little body hair, but sculpted and sexy. Kevin even had a dusting of freckles on his chest. His nipples beaded.

"Am I good enough?" Kevin asked.

"Always." He nudged Kevin to the cushions and licked his nipples.

"Oh. Wow." Kevin forked his fingers into Shaun's hair. He writhed beneath Shaun. "That feels good."

Going to get better, too. He sucked one nipple into his mouth and pinched the other nipple.

Kevin groaned.

God, he was glad he'd waited for this, but wished they hadn't waited so long. He slipped one hand to Kevin's fly and popped the button. In seconds, he had his lover's pants open. He stuffed his fingers beneath the waistband of his shorts and found his prize. He stroked Kevin's shaft, eliciting another groan.

"Shaun." Kevin tugged harder. He bucked against Shaun's hand. "Oh my God."

Shaun switched his attention to Kevin's other nipple and flicked his tongue in time with his strokes. He wanted Kevin right on the edge. He was too caught up on Kevin and couldn't think straight himself. The passion swarmed around him. He dragged his nose along Kevin's sternum, then down to his navel.

Kevin spread his legs, giving Shaun more access.

Shaun stopped touching Kevin long enough to leave the couch. "Supplies? Plus, I want you naked."

"Drawer." Kevin scrambled out of his shorts and boxers. He reclined on the sofa, his cock bobbing and pointing to the ceiling as he moved.

Such a sexy man. Long and lean with the perfect runner's shape. Kevin had just enough curls at the base of his cock to be rugged. His ribs showed when he flexed, and he mesmerized Shaun.

"Getting supplies? Or am I getting them for you?" Kevin stroked his dick.

"Yeah." Duh. He'd forgotten he'd planned to grab a rubber and lube. He checked the drawer. Just as Kevin had said, the items were there. "Do you always keep these here? Aren't you worried someone might find them on accident?"

"No, because I planned ahead." Kevin grinned. "Call it hope."

"I'm glad you did."

"But I don't keep them there all the time. You're special." The light in Kevin's eyes flashed. He splayed his legs. "Can't blame a guy for hoping."

"No, I can't." He left the couch and placed the condom and lube on the floor, then knelt next to the sofa. "I've been thinking about this all day." He stroked Kevin's dick. The feel of him turned Shaun on. He blew along his lover's shaft, then flicked his tongue across the blunt head of Kevin's cock. The taste of precum slid over his tongue. *Salty.* He swallowed Kevin deep. When Kevin groaned, Shaun hummed around him.

Kevin threaded his fingers into Shaun's hair. The bit of pain added to Shaun's pleasure. He met Kevin's gaze as he bobbed his head.

Kevin moaned and pulled harder. "Yes."

He reached up along Kevin's torso to pinch his lover's nipple.

"Holy fuck." Kevin pushed on Shaun's head, guiding him. He moved his hips, jamming his dick in and out of Shaun's mouth.

Shaun hummed again. He loved being dominated, even if just in small ways. He swallowed his lover, then flattened his tongue and laved along the underside of Kevin's shaft. He fondled his boyfriend's sac.

"Shaun." Kevin writhed beneath him. "You're making me crazy."

Shaun lost himself in the thrill of licking Kevin. He learned every ripple and nuance of him—from the thatch of dark curls at the base of his erection to the sprinkling of freckles on his hip. When Kevin moaned, Shaun eased his hand between Kevin's ass cheeks and fondled his hole.

"Oh damn." Kevin tensed. "Yes, more."

Shaun swatted at the floor for the lube. He wanted Kevin nice and open for him. He popped the lid on the bottle, then dribbled the fluid onto his fingers. Once they were nice and slick, he pushed his middle finger into Kevin's tight hole.

Kevin trembled. He held on to the cushion with one hand and tugged on Shaun's hair with the other.

Shaun drew circles around Kevin's asshole, toying with him before he pushed into his body again. He memorized the delicate ripple of Kevin's tender skin, the taste of him on his tongue and the tickle of his curls against Shaun's nose. He slid his tongue along Kevin's slit.

Each groan and whimper coming from Kevin spurred Shaun on. He eased his finger back into Kevin. *So tight.* God, he loved this. He worked his digit in and out, prepping Kevin.

"Shaun." Kevin arched his back more and his nipples beaded. His chest flushed and he panted.

Shaun moved his finger in time with his licking. He needed Kevin to come apart. Needed him to crave him. When Kevin bore down on him, Shaun added another finger.

"God, I love the burn." Kevin writhed more. He bucked his hips. "Shaun."

He didn't have Kevin quite there yet. He pumped faster, then licked his way to Kevin's balls. He sucked one testicle into his mouth. *So good.* He buried his nose against Kevin's shaft.

"Shaun." His legs wobbled and planted his foot on the cushion. "I'm so there."

Almost ready. Shaun let go of Kevin's testicle with a *pop*, then returned his attention to Kevin's dick. He lapped the pre-cum. "Come for me," Shaun murmured. "Do it." He resumed sucking on his boyfriend.

Kevin trembled and bucked. He tipped his head back. "Shaun." Shaun's name sounded so brittle when Kevin spoke. Kevin jerked into Shaun's mouth, pushing himself to the back of Shaun's throat. A strangled cry emanated from Kevin.

Shaun lapped at him, accepted everything. *Sticky, salty and perfect.* He kept working his finger in and out of Kevin, slower, but rhythmic as Kevin relaxed around him.

"Oh, my God." Kevin sagged on the cushion. "Shaun." He panted. "I can't think straight."

Good. Shaun licked his lips and sat back on his heels. "Do you want me?"

Kevin opened his legs. "More than my next breath. Fuck me."

Shaun withdrew his finger, then stood. He stripped in record time, not caring where he discarded his clothes. He opened the condom wrapper. Christ, he was already hard. He wouldn't need long before he came. He stroked himself, then donned the rubber.

Kevin reached for him. "Come here." Love shimmered in his eyes and warmth filled his smile.

"Ready?" Shaun added more lube, coating his dick. He dribbled the slippery fluid over Kevin's hole.

Another groan erupted from Kevin. He held his knees to his chest and sighed. "Going to be good."

"Yeah?" He lined his dick up with Kevin's hole. In one thrust, he pushed past the tight ring of muscle and penetrated Kevin to the hilt. *So snug.* Shaun met Kevin's gaze. The reassurance in his eyes helped—Kevin was with him.

Kevin whimpered. "So good."

He agreed. Shaun braced his knees on the couch and one hand on the back of the sofa as he began to thrust. He moved in and out, slowly to start, then he built into a steady cadence. The sound of skin on skin seemed so loud in the air.

Kevin let go of his left leg and grasped Shaun's arm. He bucked, welcoming Shaun deeper into him.

Heat started low in Shaun's belly. His limbs tingled and his thoughts blurred. The only thing that mattered right now was this moment. Kevin was the center of his universe.

A shudder rocked Kevin. He gritted his teeth. "Uh…" He dug his blunt nails into Shaun's arm.

"Fuck, come with me." Shaun trembled. It wasn't like he could hold back—not now. He increased the speed of his thrust and lost himself in the excitement of fucking Kevin. His movements turned feral. He curled over Kevin and kissed him. "Come for me."

Kevin let go of Shaun's arm and toyed with his balls. Pink infused his cheeks and he whimpered.

"Let go," Shaun murmured against Kevin's mouth. "Do it." He couldn't hold back.

Kevin gasped and stroked hard on his cock. "Shaun."

Feeling Kevin tighten around him again and seeing the pure bliss in his face pushed Shaun over the edge.

He surged into him, fucking Kevin hard and fast. His resistance shredded and the orgasm washed over him. His entire body seemed to float. He sank into Kevin and kissed him hard.

"Wow." Kevin let go of his leg and embraced Shaun. "Mind. Blown."

Shaun slowed, then pulled out and stretched on top of him. Kevin's breath warmed his skin. "You said it."

Kevin panted. "Holy shit."

Shaun pressed his face to Kevin's throat. "Uh-huh." He still couldn't think straight. Instead, he seemed to be floating—or at least it felt true.

"You're staying over tonight, yes?" Kevin petted Shaun's hair. "I want you to stay."

"Yes." He couldn't go if he tried." Take me to bed."

"We had sex." Kevin chuckled. "And you're holding me down."

"Sorry," Shaun said. "You're so perfect to hold." He climbed off him and strode to the kitchen to remove the condom.

Kevin stood and held out his hand when Shaun returned. Once Shaun twined their fingers, Kevin directed him to the bedroom.

Shaun collapsed on the bed. His muscle ached and his bell was full, but his heart was light. He had Kevin. He couldn't ask for more.

* * * *

Kevin hurried around the apartment, picking up the clothes and ensuring the door was locked. He checked to be sure he had his keys, wallet and phone accounted for, then turned off the lights and carried the clothes to the bedroom.

"You're such a neat freak." Shaun propped himself up on his elbow. "Nerdy, too, but I like it. I need someone to encourage me to clean up after myself."

He tossed the clothes onto the chair, then slid into bed. "Just remember, I will clean the toilet, but it's not my favorite chore."

Shaun reclined on the bed. "Ah, you get to be the housekeeping." He waited until Kevin was in bed with him and tangled in his embrace before he spoke. "I'm all for sharing the chores, so I'm fine with cleaning the toilet."

"Good." Kevin twined their legs, then sighed. "Bet you never thought you'd share your bed with me and my cat."

"I sort of had a feeling it'd happen." Shaun kissed Kevin's knuckles. "I don't mind. He's part of your family and he doesn't understand he's being pushy. As far as he's concerned, he belongs here."

"It's his bed when I'm at work."

"See?" Shaun petted Leo. "I hope he likes me."

"He does. If he didn't, he would've bitten you by now, and he hasn't.'" Kevin admired how Leo and Shaun got on together. They were like a little family.

"Why did you and Kyle split up? Really?" Shaun asked. "You're a good guy."

"He's not?" *God.* He'd known he'd be asked this, but that didn't make the confessional any easier.

"Seriously? I don't want to make mistakes," Shaun said. "I don't want to mess this up."

"We will."

"You're so positive."

Kevin shrugged. "What I mean is that we're going to screw things up. Things are going along fine right now, but it'll get bumpy. It's life."

"True."

"It's how we deal with the bumps — that's the thing," Kevin said. "Kyle didn't get over anything. He didn't do anything wrong — that was his mentality. He was always right and everyone else was wrong. I tended to be wrong the most and he called me on it."

Shaun frowned and said nothing.

"We had issues. Jesus. He wanted me in designer stuff and I couldn't afford it. I didn't have the extra for fancy clothes and clubbing on my salary, plus labels mean nothing to me. To him, the brand name is everything. I hated the unwarranted expense. That drove him crazy. Then, when I didn't follow his orders on how I dressed and acted, he'd get angry. You saw him when he's upset. He's mean. He lies. He starts trouble. After a while, I couldn't take it."

"So you left?"

"He moved out." Kevin shorted. "He said I was a shitty person and I should die. He said I'd never be loved and I'd end up alone." His voice cracked. He'd never wanted to discuss this or tell anyone how he'd been verbally abused. The embarrassment nearly killed him. "Sorry. I wasn't the best boyfriend. I worked long hours and didn't want to go out. Plus, I'd make him clean the apartment. I hated having to follow him to keep the apartment straight, but he left a hot mess everywhere he went."

"Kev, you're more than he ever knew and you didn't deserve that. It's natural to want your partner to help around the apartment. Honey, he screwed up. I don't know if he'll ever be loved, but you will. You'll be adored," Shaun said. "I won't have it any other way."

"You won't?" He petted Leo faster. The pent-up frustration boiled to the surface. "Shaun?"

"I won't." Shaun held him. "I'm sure this won't be perfect, but we'll do our best and I guarantee I won't treat you like he did. Ever."

He nodded. Shaun couldn't promise forever, but they had a chance.

"Sleep. I want to hold you. The night's been everything I ever wanted." Shaun cuddled up to Kevin. "My guy."

Kevin allowed himself to rest. No worries, no concerns or cares. Just bliss.

Chapter Seven

The morning after Shaun stayed over the first time, he lingered for breakfast and kissed Kevin senseless. The heat from those kisses seared Kevin to his core, even three days later. He headed to the stadium for the Saturday game, but every cell in his body wanted to be with Shaun again. They'd have to wait until Sunday, but he'd do that. He'd live.

He locked his car and strode into the building. *Just let them win so we can catch up.*

Kevin plunked everything but his work phone into his locker. Nedra was waiting for him in the kitchen. She waved to him.

"Sunny Vale is here," she said. "I don't know why, but I heard a rumor he bought the team. He wants to see you and won't even let Kyle come down here — not that Kyle should be here, but he was kicked out."

"What *was* Kyle doing in the concessions area?" Kevin donned an apron. "He's promo and rejected my requests for fresh signage."

"I don't know, but the rumor about Kyle is that he wanted to discuss you and that handsome guy from the paper. I'm guessing he's jealous." She pointed to the office. "Vale's in there. Good luck—whatever it's for."

"Thanks." He knocked on the office door. "Sir?"

"Open." Sunny Vale, car salesman extravaganza, C-grade celebrity and former mayor of Cedarwood, now owner of the Wildcats, sat behind Kevin's desk. The man had more money than God and his celebrity status might help bring people into the park, if nothing else. *Does he really own the team now?* "I wasn't sure what time you'd be in."

"I'm a bit early." Kevin nodded. "You need to see me?"

"I do. Is this your office or what?"

"It's the central office and break room. It started off as my office, but I was never in it and we needed a break room, so this is what it morphed into." He gestured to the snack machine. "It's not exciting, but it's ours. We can eat from the concessions stands, but we have to wait until everyone else has left or bring our own food. Mr. Mulhenney wanted to pinch pennies."

"It's smart to be frugal, but there should be a proper dining space and better means for the workers to eat. I'm changing the procedures. You can order one lunch from the concessions and sit in any available seats in the stadium while on breaks."

"Thank you, sir." Kevin couldn't wait to tell everyone. "That'll be in writing?"

"Of course." Mr. Vale folded his arms. "I'm told you have some suggestions for promotions. What did you want and what are those plans?"

He'd been shot down before and expected it again, but tried anyway. "I'd like to do specials. Monday is fifty-cent popcorn, Tuesday would be buy a hot dog and soda and get the cotton candy cone for free, Wednesday would be sweet tooth day with all candies half price, Thursday would be dollar beer — not the huge beers, but a smaller version — for a buck, with Friday being dollar dog and soda night, and Saturday would feature two-dollar fries."

"Sunday?"

"Bag of peanuts for a buck. It gets people in even when we're losing. People love deals," Kevin said. "I asked for new signage for each day, some banners to publicize all the deals and the ability to change out the signs for each game. We still have a third of the season left. We might not be great, but it'd help draw crowds in." He sucked in a ragged breath and waited for the owner's answer.

"I like it."

"You do?" Kevin blurted.

"I do. The ideas are stout and we should've been doing them before now. Do we have family packs?" Mr. Vale asked. "I've seen them, haven't I?"

"We did. You got four dogs, four sodas, two orders of fries and two cotton candy cones for twenty dollars. It was extremely popular. In conjunction with the family four pack of tickets, we'd sell out the family section. Mr. Mulhenney wanted to sell the tickets separately because we made more money on single tickets. The thing is, when the people buy the pack, they don't tend to just purchase those four hot dogs and such. They go back and get a second soda or a bag of peanuts. We did make some profit on the deal."

"Then we're bringing it back." Mr. Vale nodded. "I can't afford to get you more staff just yet, but let's invest in your ideas — the promotion each day and the signage will draw people in. We'll keep the concession stands that are open that way and work towards reopening the closed ones. Think you can helm it? I'll get the signs done and you rally the workers. Yes?"

"Deal." Kevin paused. "Then you really did buy the club?"

"As soon as I heard Mulhenney wanted out, I lobbied everyone I could think of and a few I didn't think could help me to get the club. It worked, and here I am." Mr. Vale stood. "I don't know what the hell we were doing for promotions, but that's my next stop. I'm assuming you know the guy. Mr. Beglin? Real piece of work. I don't know what he's spending the promotions money on, but it's not butts in seats."

"I'm not sure." He couldn't lie and had no clue what Kyle might have spent the money on. "And yes, I do know him."

"I see." Mr. Vale rounded the desk. "You should have an office, but we'll sort out a better break room, too." He clapped Kevin on the shoulder. "You're an asset to the team. You're smart and not too quick to agree to stuff. I like that you're honest with me."

"I try, sir." Kevin smiled. "We have a double-header today, so there will be a run on everything. I need to get out there to help. By the second inning of the first game, we'll be hopping."

"Good. I like to see busy workers." Mr. Vale walked out of the office. "I'll be giving everyone a copy of the new handbook and outlining exactly what I expect from them. I'll also be giving a speech tomorrow to let them know I did buy the team. I see how rampant gossip is around here." He grinned. "No different than being the mayor. Everyone wants your attention and they all want to kiss your ass to get what they want."

"I've never run for office." *And have no desire to do so.*

"Good. It'll wear you down," Mr. Vale said. "I'll see you later to check on things."

"Sure. Thank you." He couldn't wrap his mind around what had just happened. He'd been listened to and had managed to improve the situation. *Holy shit.* He couldn't wait to tell Shaun. "Thank you."

"Welcome." Mr. Vale walked out of the office and turned to Kevin. "I checked up on all my workers. I'm not making huge changes here, but I need to know the people I have are going to do their job. You know? I need to be sure I can count on you."

"You can, sir." He just wanted to do a good job and help the concessions run smoothly.

"You're the head of concessions. I want briefings and stats every day after a game." Mr. Vale shook hands with Kevin. "I'll send out a breakdown of jobs, but we're hitting the ground running right now and the briefings start on Monday."

"Thank you. I won't let you down."

"I know you won't." Mr. Vale winked, then clapped him on the shoulder before he walked away.

Kevin stared at Mr. Vale's retreating form. *Well, shit.* He knew what he'd heard and what he'd been told, but everything hadn't sunk in yet. The miracle he'd wanted had happened.

Nedra touched his arm. "Are you okay?"

"Yeah." Kevin chuckled. "We've been bought by Mr. Sunny Vale and he respects us. We're getting new signs and so forth, we're allowed and encouraged to run specials and we've got his backing." He sighed and met her gaze. "We got what we want."

"No kidding?"

"No kidding." Kevin turned to her. "So, first things first. Saturdays will be two-dollar fries for the special. Both games. Make a note for the cashiers. If anyone questions, send them to me."

"Will do." Nedra grinned, then turned on her heel. She left him to his prep work.

Kevin washed his hands and donned gloves. Once done, he focused on getting supplies out, then running onions through the chopper. His heart lightened. Things were finally going his way.

Half an hour later, Kevin took a break long enough to text Shaun from his personal phone.

Not a promotion per se, but got a lot more respect from the new team owner. Who knew? He listened to me and put promos in place.

He hit Send, then added a second text.

Will call you after the second game. Miss you.

He almost added a heart, but changed his mind. Too soon. Besides, Shaun had to know he was falling for him. God, it was so obvious.

His phone pinged with a text from Shaun.

So proud of you. Didn't know about new owner until today. Think you could get a break and see me if I come up to watch part of the game?

He hadn't thought about it. Kevin checked his watch. If Shaun came up and sat in the lower tier, he could sneak away for a few minutes to see him.

He sent a reply.

Try to get a seat in the lower tier, west end and I'll bust tail to see you.

Seconds after he sent the message, another one showed up.

Deal. Miss you, too.

Kevin tucked his phone back into his locker and grinned at his reflection. He looked like a man in love. Was he? Possibly. He cared about Shaun and could see him as his partner, but also as his lover. He missed being in Shaun's arms, craved his kiss, the way he sighed in his sleep and how he liked Leo.

This just might be love.

For the next forty-five minutes, Kevin completed his work and manned the central concessions counter. His thoughts never wandered far from Shaun. He was lucky to have Shaun in his life. He wasn't destined to be alone or treated like dirt. Shaun was his equal.

Kevin switched out the money drawer for a fresh one. He'd count the full drawer between games and after he locked it up in the safe. Part of him wanted Shaun to show up, but the rest of him was glad he hadn't arrived yet, because he had no time to stop and visit.

"Kev?" Nedra elbowed him as he came back from the office and safe. "You have a customer."

"I do?" When he rounded the corner, he spotted Shaun at the counter. "Hi."

"May I get some food?" Shaun asked. "I'm starving."

Nedra grinned. "I'll handle him. You wash your hands and take a break. If I need you, I'll holler, but I doubt that'll happen."

"Yeah." Kevin had to piece through what she'd said. *Right. Wash hands.* He shook his head, then washed his hands and left the counter. He walked out to the concourse and spotted Shaun. "Hey you." He settled in the seat beside Shaun. "Is anyone sitting here?"

"You are." Shaun tucked his cup into the built-in holder, then rested his carton of nachos on his lap and palmed Kevin's thigh. "I got tired of typing up advertisements and wanted to see you. You're right — you're not so busy when they're on a winning streak."

"You people-watched?" He hadn't had a chance to watch for Shaun. "I guess it's not that hard, though."

"It's something to do. You, though, are electric." Shaun shifted in his seat. "I miss holding you."

He couldn't stay out for too long, but didn't want to interrupt their moment. "I miss being held."

"I'm going to start looking for a house," Shaun said. "It's time."

Kevin froze. *What a hell of a topic change.* "What prompted that?"

"The roots thing we talked about. I want to put them down, and it's time. I want you to help me," Shaun said. "I looked at a couple of houses listed online and I want your input."

"Shaun?" Seemed a bit fast to be choosing houses, but whatever.

"I'm thinking about my future and the one I want to share with you." Shaun nodded and squeezed Kevin's thigh. "Kev, I'm falling for you. Why not make some moves that'll help with that future?"

He opened and closed his mouth without answering because the words evaporated. His breath clogged in his throat.

"How about you say you'll help me?" Shaun rubbed Kevin's thigh. "I know I'm going fast, but I also know this is the move I need to make. I can't keep living in an apartment because it's too easy. I'm the kind of guy that when I hit a snag, I want to run. If I have a house and admit what I want — you — I won't have a reason to run. I'll have something that's mine. I'm too old to be goofing around. Things will be easy with us, but hard too, and I'm okay with that. I want the rough, the smooth, the whole thing with you."

"You're asking me to move in with you, aren't you?" He wanted to follow Shaun's way of thinking, but Jesus, he couldn't keep it all straight. He wasn't sure he wanted to move in with anyone — if that was what he was being asked. It might be nice to live together. They'd have nights together and could see each other at the end of the day, but they'd have nowhere to run if they had an argument.

"Not yet. I move at warp speed, but not all the time." Shaun sipped his drink, then grinned. "I want us to have a chance to feel this all out, but I want a house. I'm tired of living in a tiny box apartment. This is something I want, and the more places I look at, the more it feels right."

"Okay." He respected Shaun's decision.

"But enough about houses. You've got mad respect here. Your co-worker couldn't say enough about you." Shaun massaged Kevin's inner thigh. "It's great."

"Yeah." He stared at Shaun for another minute, then remembered what he'd wanted to tell Shaun in the first place. "I guess I do. Nedra likes me, though. She's always had my back." He laughed. "But this new owner, Mr. Vale, is suitable, I suppose. He was a decent enough mayor and an okay celebrity, but he's got a good head for business—better than Mulhenney, the former team owner. I know Vale's letting me try out my ideas to sell food at better prices and hopefully move more of it. If we can get people in and sell our concessions at a decent, affordable price, then fine by me."

"You will. He's got an asset in you." Shaun bumped shoulders with him. "I'm impressed with your job and your ability to do it. You're really someone special."

"You are, too." He kissed Shaun. "The ninth inning is about to start. Our relief pitcher seems to be a better closer than starting player. It's good because he's getting the opposing team's players out faster, but it means the game goes faster and cuts down my time to clean up before the next game. The two-hour break isn't always enough."

"Then go. I'm looking forward to your texts tonight. Dirty is good," Shaun said. "I love a dirty text."

The tips of Kevin's ears burned. He'd never sent a dirty text. Ever. Then again, he might have to try. "I will."

"Good." Kevin left his seat. "Until later."

"Until later." Shaun winked. "I've got to finish these nachos and watch the rest of the game. I'll probably let the crowd thin out before I go, too. I hate traffic."

"Sounds good." He waved, then leaned in to kiss Shaun again. "Bye." He wanted to say more, but held back instead. He waved before he made his way to the concession stands. When he entered the staff portion of the stand, Nedra groaned.

"Good. We need you," she said. "You've got a good guy. Has to be, because this is the first time you've returned to the stand with a smile on your face. I like it."

"I do, too." Kevin jumped into the swing of things and tried to keep his mind off Shaun. The house thing bothered him, but all-in-all, his heart was lighter and his spirits soared. Nedra was right. He was in a positive mood — partially because of the job changes, but mostly because of Shaun.

The house idea was a huge thing and scary, but could be what they both needed. He saw a future with Shaun, too, and a little house — one with a yard — might be the piece they needed to make their relationship complete.

* * * *

Shaun waited in his seat until the game concluded and the crowd thinned. By the time he walked past the concession stand, the garage-type door had been pulled down. *Closed.* So much for one last chat with Kevin.

He made his way through the stadium. The noise of the game was gone and the excitement of the experience had died, too. The smells of the food lingered in the air. The flags flapped in the breeze and Shaun understood the thrill of being at the ballpark. The energy in the crowd had been palpable. He missed the electricity. It wasn't quite as exciting as being with Kevin, but nothing compared to his boyfriend. Kevin fascinated him. He had no idea how Kevin managed to keep all the orders straight. He'd mix everything up, while Kevin took the chaos of the concession stand in stride.

Shaun wandered out to his car. Instead of driving straight home, he opted to locate the houses he'd looked at online. Each of the homes had something in common — three bedrooms — enough for an office and guest room — two bathrooms, a two-car garage and especially a large back yard. Two of the homes ranked high on his list because they featured tall fenced-in yards or privacy shrubs. He liked the layout of the third house, but it didn't have a large yard or two-car garage — but there was room to add on. Did he want the headache of home improvements? *Not yet.*

He'd have to show the houses to Kevin and do some walk-throughs. *Not impossible.*

Shaun drove into the parking lot of his apartment. Once he parked and gathered his things, he locked the car and headed up to his unit. He wanted a bigger place, but the smallness of his one-bedroom apartment became glaringly obvious. It wasn't just small. It was cramped. Time for something new.

He turned on his tablet and sent an email to Tony, the realty guru at the newspaper. If anyone would know what to do, it would be him. Shaun needed help navigating the housing market. After he wrote and sent the email, he headed to the bathroom for a shower. He should've run today, but he'd rather veg a while and run with Kevin tomorrow.

He also should've called Cheryl to let her know he was still alive. She'd want to know and want updates on Kevin. Calling her wouldn't be a short chat. She liked to talk — then again, so did he. If he wanted to accomplish anything else while he waited on Kevin, he'd have to call her later.

He wondered how long Kevin would be at the stadium tonight, though. A while, probably, since the second game didn't start until seven. He checked the clock. Six-fifty-five.

Kevin would be a long while and he'd have time to call Cheryl.

His phone rang and Shaun checked the ID, hoping it was Kevin. Not his lover. Not even Cheryl. His heart lodged in his throat.

His ex-partner, Jonah.

Shit. He hadn't heard from his ex in over a year. What could Jonah possibly want? He should let the call go to voicemail. At one time, he'd loved Jonah. Sure, they'd parted on okay terms, but still. He'd had his heart broken when Jonah had brought around his new boyfriend before he and Jonah had split.

His phone silenced and he allowed himself to breathe. He hadn't realized he'd been holding his breath. Maybe the call was a misdial.

Shaun sagged in his seat. He'd wondered more than a few times what he'd feel like if he ever ran into Jonah again. Would he be worried? Concerned? Drawn to him all over again? The love hadn't faded?

He wasn't sure, but if his initial reaction was anything, then the love was gone.

His phone rang again. *Jonah.*

Shaun sucked in a ragged breath and swiped to answer. *Just get it over with.* "Hello?" He'd once cared about this man and wanted to marry him. How could he just ignore him now? Easy. Jonah wanted to move on with his life and didn't care about it. If he did, he had a strange way of showing it.

"Hi," Jonah said. "How are you?"

"Good. You?" His voice wobbled. *Damn it.* He couldn't show any weakness. "Is everything all right?"

They hadn't spoken since the split. Why wait this long to call? "You don't talk unless you want something."

"I needed to hear your voice — that's what I wanted."

"You did?" Shaun asked. Jonah hadn't said things like that when they were together. Jonah wasn't the romantic type — unless he wanted to get someone into bed.

"Yeah." Jonah chuckled. "We were together for a long time and I do miss you. I miss how it feels to have someone in the house, to know you're on the other end of the phone line, to kiss you when I've had a rough day…the little stuff."

"That's…yeah." He hated sounding indecisive. "You do?"

"It's not like we parted hating each other," Jonah said. "It wasn't great, but it wasn't bad, and I have fond memories of you. I look back at what we had and it makes me smile."

Shaun wouldn't say that. Since the last year of their relationship, he wasn't Jonah's biggest fan. Most of the time, he couldn't stand being in the same room with him. "Sort of. It was pleasant." *Ish.* He paused. "You told me you hoped I'd end up falling in front of a bus and I'd never find love again."

"I was angry and that was harsh. I'm sorry."

Sorry? Jonah had to be dying. He never apologized for anything. "Uh, okay." *Christ.* This was harder than he'd ever imagined. "Did you need something? It's not like you to wander down memory lane."

"I'm finding in my older age that I do like to reminisce. I'm not a total shallow jerk, you know. While going through my stuff, I found some photographs that are yours. They're of your parents when they were married. I think one is a wedding photo," Jonah said. "I assumed you'd want them. You do, right?"

"I'd like them, yes." He'd lost those photographs when he and Jonah had broken up. Having the pictures back would be nice, but the timing didn't add up. "Where did you find them?"

"In one of the hutch drawers."

Interesting. He didn't keep his pictures in the hutch. *"When* did you find them?"

"About a month ago. I wanted to send them, but I worried they'd get lost in the mail. You know how things are," Jonah said. "It wasn't safe, so I hesitated. I'd feel terrible if I mailed them, texted you they were on the way and they never made it. All those memories…poof."

"That makes sense and I appreciate your kindness. The mail has been slow lately." Somehow, though, he doubted Jonah's story. He could've sent them via the specialty mail services and had them tracked. "Then how are you going to ensure I get them back?"

"I wanted to meet up to give them to you in person. I'm going to assume there are coffee shops where you are, right?" Jonah asked. "Where are you now?"

"Cedarwood. I followed Mom up here and got a job." He'd forgotten he hadn't mentioned to Jonah where he'd moved. He'd severed that part of his life and until now hadn't wanted to revisit it.

"I knew you would go with your mom. You're so close to her," Jonah said. "How is your mother? Are you seeing anyone? I haven't seen you out and wondered."

"Mom's fine, but she's doing her thing. We don't talk much, but I am seeing someone—his name is

Kevin." He'd bet this was why Jonah wanted to see him. He wanted to get nosy.

"Older? Younger?"

Is it any of your business? "My age." Jonah liked to lord the fact he was older than Shaun over his head.

"Ah. Does he love you?"

His irritation rose. "It's still new, but yeah." He wasn't lying. The passion between them was strong and he believed it was love.

"Ah, so you're living together and fucking like rabbits. Does he know you're talking to me? That you still have my number in your phone?" Jonah asked.

"Stop." He wasn't in the mood for this shit.

"Come on, Shaun. Be honest. Why not delete me? I'll bet he doesn't know your secrets."

He'd had enough. Jonah could be a manipulative shit when he wanted to and this wasn't the time to push. "First, I want my pictures back, and I'll meet you in Ashland at the truck stop to get them. As for Kevin, we're good. We are in a great place and happy, so don't ruin it. Got me? Don't be this way."

Jonah snorted. "Who says I'm being *that way*? I just asked," he said. "When do you want to meet?"

"How about Wednesday? I'm available after three." He just wanted to get this over with.

"Four on Wednesday. I'll be there," Jonah said. "Should I wait in the car or inside? I don't want you to be disgusted by seeing me."

"Wait in the food court." Jonah would have to add the little derogatory comments. The ass.

"We used to be good together, Shaun," Jonah said. "We used to make each other happy. Where did we go wrong?"

"You wanted to sleep around."

"I never wanted to get married," Jonah said. "You assumed the sleeping-around part. You never asked me for clarification."

Shaun thanked God he was sitting down. Jonah's declaration would've knocked him over if he hadn't been seated. "Wait. You had a boyfriend and I remember meeting him."

"You did, but not until after we split."

Not true.

"I didn't invite you to meet him until after we were done because I wanted to know it was the truth," Jonah said.

Something didn't feel right. He remembered meeting a guy—Stephen or Karl, or maybe it was Dave—but he and Jonah hadn't split yet. He recalled the guy coming over to the house they were renting and Jonah explaining Shaun and the man should be friends.

"Yeah, I thought you'd forget," Jonah said. "I want to see you. I miss you and miss us. It'd be good to have a bit of time together."

"I suppose." Closure would be nice. "Just be there on Wednesday." He'd have to tell Kevin soon. He doubted Kevin would be upset, but still. They had to be open with each other. Jonah was his past and Kevin was his future. He was starting to understand what love was and it defined his feelings for Kevin.

"I'll see you and I will bring the photos," Jonah said. "Bye, Shaun."

"Bye." He hung up. Shaun closed his eyes and rested his head against the cushion. *Well, fuck.* He'd thought Jonah was out of his life. Thought he'd moved on, but Jonah had found a way to pull him back in. That was Jonah, though. He lived for the push-pull. One day he never wanted to see Shaun again, then the next he missed Shaun.

Jonah probably did have photographs and could be acting nice enough to give them back, but the story didn't make sense. If Jonah knew about the photos, had he really found them a month ago? Why not call before now? When he and Jonah were together at the end of their relationship, they couldn't be in the same room at the same time because Jonah had thought he was fucking every other guy there.

He rubbed his forehead. He and Jonah did want different things. Jonah wanted to be with everyone and his actions spoke to his desires. For someone who said he hadn't been sleeping around, why had Shaun found him in bed with someone else three different times?

He shoved the phone away and closed his eyes. Why did his ex want to fuck with him?

Because Jonah can.

Shaun sighed. He wished he were at Kevin's so he could pet Leo. The cat gave him comfort. Plus, it meant he'd be there to see Kevin when he got home.

He groaned. *Fuck.* He needed to tell Kevin right now about Jonah. He slapped for the phone, then grabbed the device. He should check the score to see if Kevin would even be available. What was the schedule for the team like on Wednesday? Maybe Kevin could come with him.

He scrolled through the remaining dates. *Shit.* A game on the meeting day. Hopefully Kevin wouldn't care about the quick meet-up and would give him strength.

Shaun left the sofa and made himself a snack. He wasn't hungry, but needed to eat something. Once he returned to the living room, he turned on the stereo.

Right now, he needed music to soothe his soul. His phone buzzed with a new email.

He tapped the icon to check the message. It was from Tony, the realtor. According to the message, he'd been given time slots to view each of the five houses he'd sent inquiries in for and Tony would be happy to help him.

At least something was going right. He spent the next hour talking with Tony about the tours and house buying. He knew what he wanted in a home and how much he wanted to spend. Now that he had a plan, he couldn't wait to get started and tell Kevin. Home buying was turning out to be a strange but interesting journey.

His phone buzzed and he retrieved the new message as well as the charging cord. He plugged in the device. His spirits lifted. A text from Kevin.

He settled on the sofa.

Miss you.

Shaun grinned.

Miss you, too. Good game?

Kevin replied in seconds.

Good enough. Kept it close, but we lost.

Damn. They'd been ahead when he'd looked last.

Bet you're tired.

Kevin's reply came almost as quick as if they were talking on the phone.

Exhausted, but I miss you. Can't sleep without talking to you.

No? Shaun rubbed his chin. He liked knowing Kevin was just as caught up as he'd become in just a short period of time.

Are you home?

Kevin replied a moment later.

No. Taking 5 in the break room. Needed a breather. I'll leave in 45.

Ah. He could work with that.

Mind if I come over?

Kevin didn't reply right away and Shaun wondered for a split second if he'd overstepped.

Yes. Please?

Shaun sagged in his seat and exhaled the breath he hadn't realized he'd been holding.

You're sure?

He needed to know he wasn't pushing.

I want you there. Need you.

He clutched the phone and his desire for Kevin rose.

I'll be there. I'll relive your tension.

He'd pack a bag in a moment and meet Kevin in the parking lot of his apartment.

You're the best stress relief because you calm me.

Kevin's reply made Shaun's day. His heart belonged to Kevin. God, he'd fallen hard for him. He sent two texts to Kevin.

You make me feel like me. See you in a little while.

<3

He didn't care that he'd texted a heart. Kevin was his person and he wanted everyone to know it was love. He couldn't wait to see him. Right now, he needed to be loved and cherished. He wanted to prove his devotion to Kevin, too. He'd become a better man because of his boyfriend. He'd found his other half. Now he had to figure out how to keep him.

Chapter Eight

Kevin arrived at his apartment building and spotted Shaun's car. His heart leapt. He'd wanted to see Shaun and his desires had come true. Right now, he needed to hold him. He parked, then left his car.

Shaun remained behind the wheel of his for a moment, then opened the driver's side door. "Have you ever had one of those days?"

"I have." He ventured over to Shaun.

"I want to turn off my brain and exist. No thinking, no trying to sort other people's shit out." Shaun left the car and closed the door. "I need you."

"To do what?" Kevin grasped Shaun's hand. "Listen to you? Play therapist?"

"No." Shaun slid his arm around Kevin, then tugged him close and kissed him. Fire lit in his eyes. "To be inside you."

Kevin shivered, despite the warm, late-summer-night air. "Yes." Blood rushed to his dick and his heart beat faster. "Come with me." He dragged Shaun upstairs to his apartment. His long day had just gotten better because Shaun was there. He headed into his place, and while Shaun closed the door, Kevin ensured Leo was okay, then focused on his boyfriend.

"You made my day when you texted." He kicked out of his shoes. He tossed his wallet, keys and phones onto the counter. "I needed to see you."

"Did you?" Shaun abandoned his keys, phone and wallet with Kevin's, then wrapped him in his embrace. He crushed his mouth on Kevin's. This wasn't a slow or sweet kiss, but rather a claiming, demanding kiss. He sucked on Kevin's tongue and stole his breath.

Kevin simply went along for the ride. He breathed Shaun in, savored his taste and the way Shaun touched him.

"You're my drug," Shaun said. He pressed Kevin to the apartment door. "Need you."

"You've got me." Kevin squirmed free long enough to tug Shaun to the bedroom. "Shower with me."

"God, yes." Shaun shoved Kevin's shirt over his head. He unbuttoned Kevin's pants, barely giving him the chance to consider what was happening.

Kevin didn't care. He pushed his pants and boxers down to his ankles and stepped out of the wadded-up clothing. When he turned to twist the knob in the shower, Shaun embraced him from behind. He nibbled along Kevin's shoulder. Steam billowed as the shower water heated up.

"You smell like fries," Shaun said. He raked his teeth along Kevin's neck. "But you feel so hard and sexy. I like it."

His skin tingled. The stress washed away with each kiss and touch. He wasn't in the shower yet, but felt better than ever.

Shaun nudged Kevin's ass with the bulge in his trousers. "Want to be inside you."

"I want you inside me." He stepped into the shower. "Come on."

Shaun stripped, then filed in behind Kevin. Instead of speaking, Shaun dipped his head and turned Kevin around. He sucked on Kevin's nipple and palmed his ass as he embraced him.

"Shaun." His senses shifted into high alert.

"Love your ass," Shaun murmured. He swatted Kevin and switched his attention to the other nipple.

"Shaun." He had no other words. The water stung his shoulders and dripped down his face. He couldn't think straight. "I should wash you."

"Soon." Shaun stood tall. He gathered his dick with Kevin's and stroked them together. The water sluiced over them and the delicious sensation of cock on cock sent shivers down Kevin's spine.

Kevin added soap to give extra lubrication. Heat flowed in his veins and he grinded in Shaun's hand. The orgasm was building too fast, but fuck. This was too good to ignore. He held on to his boyfriend.

"Like that?" Shaun asked. "Want more?"

"Yes." Kevin rocked harder. Every nerve ending and synapse in his body buzzed. He fondled Shaun's balls. "More."

Shaun said nothing and dropped to his knees. He rinsed Kevin, then swallowed him to the root. He flattened his palms on Kevin's thighs. When he bobbed his head, he pushed deep before pulling back. With each plunge, he stroked Kevin's sac, adding extra sensations to the mix.

Kevin writhed, pumping his hips and fucking Shaun's mouth. His stress evaporated. He palmed the back of Shaun's head and groaned. "Shaun." He wanted to say something more intelligent, but the words were gone.

Shaun didn't speak and instead moved faster. He flattened his tongue along the underside of Kevin's erection. When he swallowed, he fried Kevin's brain cells.

"Oh fuck." Kevin jerked into his lover's mouth. His restraint snapped and he shivered again. "Shaun." The orgasm crashed within him. He pistoned into Shaun's mouth. As his climax hit full force, he tensed, then sagged forward.

Shaun bobbed his head a bit longer, then withdrew. "Are you relaxed?"

"Yes." Kevin wobbled into him when Shaun stood. "I'm great."

Shaun slid his hand around the back of Kevin's neck and kissed him. "Good. Let me wash you."

"I doubt I could manage it, even if I wanted to." His brain fogged with the power of the post-orgasmic glow.

"Sure." Shaun rubbed the cloth over his body. His nerve endings were on fire. His balls were sensitive, too. He loved being touched, and craved Shaun's dick in his ass.

"Rinse." Shaun turned him around and nudged him under the spray. He said nothing as he tucked Kevin to his chest with one arm. He scrubbed Kevin's hair with his free hand. Once he finished shampooing Kevin, he nudged him under the spray again. "All clean, you dirty man."

"Yeah." Kevin could barely think straight. He leaned into Shaun.

"Go out to your bed. I'll join you." Shaun swatted Kevin's ass as he let go of him. "I'll catch up."

"Yeah." He managed to leave the shower stall. Kevin dried off, then wandered into the bedroom. He collapsed on his bed, worn out yet jazzed. *What craziness!* He should be tired and running on fumes. With Shaun there, he wanted to stay up all night.

A moment later, Shaun strode nude into the bedroom. "You're a sexy man."

"I'm me." Kevin reached for him. "Let me get you hard." He wanted to lick his lover.

"It's still my turn." Shaun crawled onto the bed and folded him in half. "I can't get enough of your ass." He held Kevin's knees to his chest.

Kevin whimpered as Shaun dipped his head. Droplets from his damp hair landed on Kevin's abdomen. Kevin widened his legs. His entire being tingled. He writhed beneath Shaun and each time Shaun lapped at his asshole, it pushed him closer to coming apart.

Shaun dug his fingers into Kevin's calves while he swirled his tongue around Kevin's hole.

"Shaun." He panted. His legs trembled and he bore down on Shaun. The world outside failed to matter. His stresses, his concerns, meant nothing. This moment was everything. "Love it."

Shaun stroked Kevin's dick while he rimmed Kevin. Every nerve in Kevin's body was back on high alert and his focus turned solely to Shaun. A strangled cry erupted from Kevin's throat.

"More?" Shaun asked against Kevin's hole. "Need me?"

"Yes." His muscles quaked. "Fuck me."

Shaun tapped Kevin's hole with his finger. "We need stuff."

Kevin groaned. "I'm clean. Get the lube and fuck me." He'd never been this scattered in his life. Then again, he'd never thought he'd be having this conversation while in bed. The raw need overwhelmed him and he embraced his desire for Shaun. "Yes?"

"Good." Shaun toyed with Kevin's tender skin. "I'm clean, too."

"Good to know." God, he wanted Shaun in him.

Shaun tugged Kevin's shaft one more time, then left the bed. He returned with the bottle of lube. "I crave you."

Kevin opened his mouth, but no sound came out. He craved Shaun too and needed to be one with him. He flexed his hole in a silent invitation.

"Sexy." Shaun dribbled lube over Kevin's ass, then coated his own dick. "Need me?"

"Yes." For the hundredth time, yes. "Please?"

Shaun crawled on the bed. He lined his cock up with Kevin's hole and pushed. Kevin bore down on him. The burn excited Kevin. He felt alive, and groaned.

"Shaun." Kevin hooked his legs around Shaun's waist. When he looked into Shaun's eyes, he saw forever and his mind was blown. Shaun meant the world to him.

"Kevin." Shaun grasped Kevin's hips and began to thrust. He pushed deep, making them one body, before pulling most of the way out again. A fine sheen of perspiration sparkled on Shaun's shoulders. Fire lit in Shaun's eyes. He reminded Kevin of a god.

Shaun increased his pace. The bedsprings squeaked with each thrust. Kevin welcomed Shaun into his body. He memorized each ripple and unique aspect of his lover, from the mole on Shaun's cheek, to the flex of his abs and the way his legs seemed to go on forever.

When Shaun pushed deep, he massaged Kevin's prostate. Kevin's legs twitched and he reached between his thighs to stroke his own dick. He caressed himself in time with Shaun's thrusts, whipping himself into frenzy. He bucked against Shaun. The heat from his second orgasm swamped him. He fixed his gaze on Shaun. He couldn't come this fast. Not yet. He wanted to string this out and enjoy each moment.

"Mine?" Shaun asked. The pace of his thrusts increased.

"All yours." Kevin stopped fighting the orgasm. The climax washed over him and he tensed from head to toe before he groaned. "Oh fuck."

Shaun growled. He tipped his head back and pushed with abandon. "Kevin." He slammed into Kevin and his cock throbbed as he came.

Kevin relaxed. A warm rush slid over him. When he looked into Shaun's eyes this time, he was home.

Shaun slowed his thrusts, then stopped. He sagged on Kevin. "Damn."

Agreed, even if he had no words. He clung to Shaun and lowered his legs.

Shaun pulled out, but stayed on top of Kevin. He rested his head on Kevin's chest. "Your heart is pounding."

"Gave me a workout." He embraced Shaun. He wanted to come home to this — to Shaun and the little family they were creating — every night.

Shaun's breath tickled Kevin's chest. After what seemed like an eternity, Shaun spoke again. "You wore me out."

"You're staying tonight," Kevin said. It wasn't a question. "Don't go." Kevin needed Shaun beside him as he slept.

"There's no place else I'd rather be." Shaun kissed Kevin's chest. "With you." He slid beside Kevin on the bed and rested on his back. "You're the fix."

"I am? Fix for what?" Kevin tucked himself into Shaun's side. "I'm enough? Or something else?"

"You're more than enough," Shaun said. "You made me *me* again. That's the fix. I'm whole."

"I like knowing that." Kevin sighed. Sleep overwhelmed him. He yawned. "I hate to say this, but I'm worn out, too. I can't keep my eyes open."

"Then sleep. I'll be right here." Shaun left the bed long enough to grab a towel. When he returned, he wiped lube and cum from his dick, then swiped the towel over Kevin's ass. "Better." He abandoned the towel on the floor, then joined him in bed again. Shaun dragged the blankets over them. "I need a rest, too."

Kevin wanted to say more, but he truly couldn't stay awake. The day had been too much and he needed to recharge. So much of his life was structured, but a lot was out of control. One thing he knew — he'd fallen for Shaun.

* * * *

Kevin woke to Leo sprawled out on his belly and Shaun's ass grinding against his hip. What a perfect way to start the morning. Leo stared at him and purred, vibrating Kevin's chest. Kevin petted the cat, enjoying the relative quiet of the day. He didn't have to go to work until two-thirty and could enjoy his time with Shaun.

Shaun rolled onto his back. "I haven't felt this good in ages." He kissed Kevin. "Good morning, handsome."

"Good morning."

"The welcoming committee showed up." Shaun petted Leo. "Hi, guy."

Leo flicked his tail, but remained on Kevin's chest.

"He's still not sure about you," Kevin said. "You're here and this is his spot."

"With you?"

"Uh-huh."

Shaun scratched Leo behind the ears. "I like your master, Leo. I like him a lot and I want to share more than just a few moments of his time. I like you, even if you don't seem to care for me. I hope we can be friends and share Kevin. He's the kind of guy I've been looking for. May I stay?"

Kevin switched his gaze between Shaun and Leo. He hadn't had many boyfriends since the split with Kyle, but no other guys had asked Leo for permission to be with Kevin. None.

Leo sniffed Shaun's fingers, then flicked his tail again. He blinked once before he stood, then left the bed.

"Is that the seal of approval? Or at least a chance at getting it?" Shaun asked. "I can't tell. Did I say something wrong? Maybe it's morning breath."

"Morning, yes. Breath? No. He wants his breakfast." Kevin held Shaun's hand. "He needs his morning vittles so he can do whatever it is he does all day."

"How could I forget?" Shaun grinned. "Want to run today? I've got my running shoes in my trunk and a change of clothing in my bag—which is also in the trunk."

"You can go get it—the bag and shoes, not trunk." Kevin rolled onto his side and tangled his legs with

Shaun's. "I'd love a run. Let me feed Leo, you can get your stuff, then we can hydrate and go."

"And shower together after the run?" Shaun's eyes lit up. "Like last night?"

"I'm game." He had nothing to do and nowhere to go. "Why not?"

* * * *

For the next three days, Shaun ran each morning with Kevin. Guilt gnawed at him, but he couldn't find the right time to tell him about Jonah. On Wednesday morning, he returned to his apartment with Kevin. He lived for the quiet time with Kevin. Each run brought them closer together and made him feel like he belonged. But the damn trouble with Jonah lingered in his mind. How could one person be such a pain in the ass? He had no idea how to explain his ex, either.

Kevin jogged to a stop in front of Shaun's apartment. "I'm going to feel this later." He laughed. "But it's worth it. I needed to do a longer distance today. Gotta get ready for the race."

"We do." He glanced over at Kevin. Sweat slicked his chest and his muscles flexed with each breath. His hair stood out at odd angles and the sprinkling of growth on his cheeks caught the light. He leaned over, giving Shaun a great view of his tight ass.

"I feel better than I have in ages," Kevin said. "I'm not so tense at work. Nedra likes it because I'm not grumpy."

"I've heard I'm easier to deal with, too." Shaun licked his lips, then eased up behind Kevin. He slid his hands over Kevin's lower back. "We should go inside."

"Is someone watching us?" Kevin stood tall. "Someone giving us the look?"

"No." Shaun massaged Kevin's shoulder. "I can't keep my eyes off you." He kissed him hard. "Seeing you in those shorts and all sweaty has me thinking very naughty things."

Hunger shimmered in Kevin's eyes. "Like maybe what I'm thinking?"

"I'm sure it is." Shaun trailed his fingers along Kevin's spine. "Plus, it's private."

Kevin shivered. "Yes." He allowed Shaun to hold his hand as they went into the apartment building. Once in the privacy of the elevator, Kevin pinned him to the wall and kissed him. He gave Shaun no chance to think as he opened his mouth and sucked on Shaun's tongue.

Shaun roved his hands all over Kevin's ribs, then down to his ass. He brushed the bulge in his running shorts against the one in Kevin's shorts. Blood rushed to his cock and need overwhelmed him. He bit Kevin's bottom lip, then tweaked one of Kevin's nipples.

A groan rumbled in Kevin's throat as the bell rang for Shaun's floor. Shaun helped Kevin out of the elevator, but barely noticed his surroundings as he headed to his apartment. All he saw was Kevin.

His thoughts blurred. He loved the way Kevin's lip crinkled when he was deep in thought, the way he squirmed so much before he finally fell asleep or how he stared at Shaun with utter love in his eyes.

Kevin smoothed his hand over Shaun's ass. "Have I told you I love your butt? It's perfect."

Shaun fumbled with his keys and opening the apartment door. Kevin knew how to blow out his synapses. He finally unlocked the door, then nudged Kevin inside. He'd never last at this rate. Instead of his normal routine of taking off his shoes and abandoning his keys on the table, he kept the shoes on and tossed his keys onto the floor.

Kevin's eyes widened as Shaun pinned him to the door. He splayed his hands on the door and moaned when Shaun shoved his fingers beneath the waistband of his shorts.

"Want you," Shaun said against Kevin's throat. "Want your sticky, sweet, heady…I want it all. Right now."

Kevin whimpered, but didn't argue. Instead, he ground his hips and rode Shaun's thigh.

"That's it." Shaun shoved the shorts down, exposing Kevin's ass. He scraped his nails across Kevin's skin. "I want to be inside you. Is that where you want me?"

"Yes." Kevin held on to Shaun's shoulders. "Now."

"Now?" Shaun let go of his lover and turned him around, then pinned him to the door again. He yanked Kevin's shorts to his knees. "Your ass is a thing of beauty, too." He dashed away long enough to retrieve a bottle of lube. When he returned to Kevin, he sucked the side of Kevin's neck, drawing a groan from him.

Kevin managed to work his shorts down to his ankles and arched his back, baring his butt. He pressed his cheek to the door. "Fuck me."

"I will." Shaun opened the bottle of lube, then dribbled the clear fluid down the crack of Kevin's ass. He slid his finger along the slickness until he found Kevin's hole. He toyed with the tender skin. "I'm burying myself so deep in here." He eased his digit past the tight muscle. "Breathe, baby."

Kevin rocked his hips, pushing himself onto Shaun's finger. "Love that."

"Stroke yourself." Shaun added more lube and another finger. He wanted Kevin nice and loose for him. Once he got inside his lover, he wouldn't be able to stop. He sucked on Kevin's shoulder and increased pressure on Kevin's shoulder in time with moving his fingers in his lover's ass. He scissored his digits, opening Kevin.

Kevin planted one hand and his cheek on the door, then reached between his legs. He grunted. "More."

"Relax." He'd said the word, but could he do the same? *Bullshit.* He could barely think straight. "Need me?" he asked against Kevin's shoulder. "Tell me."

"Fuck me." Kevin writhed. "Oh God."

"Good boy." He withdrew his fingers, then shoved his shorts down. He added more lube, slickening his cock, then lined himself up with Kevin's hole. "All mine." He loved the heat of the moment. Frenzied. He grasped Kevin's hips and sank to the hilt into him. The feel of Kevin's snug hole and the immediacy of the moment weren't lost on Shaun. He moved slow at first, but the passion and desire in his veins took over. Nothing else mattered.

"Shaun." Kevin rocked against him. He shivered and moaned. "More."

Without a second thought, Shaun increased his pace. He pushed deep into Kevin, loving the oneness of their connection. He'd never felt anything this heady or deep with anyone else. Kevin brought out the wild side of him, but the protective side, too. He wanted a future with this man.

Shaun lost himself in the thrill of fucking Kevin. He mashed Kevin into the door, pistoning into him. Blood surged through his body and desire overwhelmed him. He gritted his teeth.

Kevin shuddered and bucked against Shaun. He met him thrust for thrust. "Oh, God."

Shaun held on to Kevin, sliding his arm around his boyfriend's waist. He grasped Kevin's hip with his other hand. "Fuck." He pressed his mouth to the back of Kevin's neck. "Fuck, fuck, fuck." He had no other words. Nothing rational, anyway. He didn't care who heard them or what anyone thought. This was raw power and love in motion.

The power of the orgasm crept into his brain. He raked his teeth over Kevin's skin. "Come for me," Shaun bit out. "Do it."

Kevin whimpered as he jutted his ass at Shaun. He tensed, then groaned and bowed his head.

Feeling Kevin come apart was more than enough to push Shaun over the edge. He tipped his head back and growled as his thrusts turned animalistic. The world around him blurred and he bared his teeth. He surged into Kevin a final time, pushing as deep as possible as he came. "Fuck."

Shaun groaned and pressed Kevin to the door. Sex had never been frantic before, but Kevin brought out his animal side. He kissed Kevin's bare shoulder. "I love you," he murmured.

Kevin tensed. "Shaun?"

He withdrew from Kevin. *Shit.* He needed a towel or something. He grabbed the towel from his gym bag and dried Kevin's back down to his ass. "I do. I love you, Kev." He cleaned up his boyfriend, then himself. "It's fast, but it's the truth."

Kevin yanked his shorts up, faced Shaun, then raked his fingers through his hair. "How do you know?"

"That I love you? Easy." He pulled his own shorts up and tossed the towel onto his bag. He couldn't have this conversation with his clothes around his ankles. "My heart aches for you when we're not together. I think about you often and I feel more like me when I'm with you. I see my future with you and I want to grow old beside you. I've never felt this way about anyone. Ever."

Kevin sighed. "You're sure?"

"I am." He curled his fingers under Kevin's chin. "I've never been more positive in my life. I know it'll take you longer to admit it, but when I look into your eyes, I know you feel it, too. No rush, but I needed to tell you how I feel." A twinge of relief hit. He'd been honest and Kevin hadn't pushed him away. Progress.

"I can accept that." Kevin nodded and rested his hands on his hips. "I thought you were going to tell me something outlandish, like you and your ex were having sex and you needed one more fling to get him out of your system. You know, something outlandish."

Shaun frowned. "Because you'd be so okay with me doing that—fucking," he said, his voice flat. "I'm joking—I know you'd hate it." *Holy fucking shit.* Kevin's comment had to be a stray guess, but still, it was too harsh. "Don't tell me you think I am. I'm not."

"If I found out you were with your ex, then it's a dealbreaker. I don't date guys who are with someone else." Kevin shrugged. "But I trust you. I don't trust many people, but I do you. I truly doubt you're dating your ex or doing anything like that, because you'd tell me." He shrugged again. "Plus, Leo would know you were doing something shady and bite you. That's how he knew Kyle was no good."

"He's never bitten me." Shaun couldn't wait any longer. He hadn't done anything wrong, but that didn't make the guilt go away. Besides, Kevin was right—he hated keeping secrets from him. "Kevin, I need to talk to you."

"Aren't you talking to me now?" He grabbed his water bottle from the floor and took a drink, then gasped. His brow crinkled. "You're in love with me. What else do I need to know? You're clean, I'm clean, you're in love with me and you're my boyfriend. What's there to know?"

"I'm meeting with Jonah this afternoon." Shaun held his breath, awaiting Kevin's reply.

"Meeting with him?" Kevin asked, his voice soft. "Like...*meeting*?"

"Yes." Shit. He'd answered that wrong. "It's complicated."

"Why?" Kevin put space between them. "Shaun?"

He couldn't keep this to himself any longer. "He called me, said he had photos that were mine and wanted to give them to me. I guess there are wedding pictures from my folks' wedding, photos of my parents and other photos I had. They were missing," he said. "If he really has the pictures, then I want them back."

"Understandable." Kevin's expression remained blank. "So you're seeing him today?"

"Yes. In Ashland. I wanted to bring you, but there's a game this afternoon." Shaun rubbed his forehead. "I'm sorry, but I want my possessions back."

"I'm sure you do."

"Yet you don't trust me," Shaun said. "You're not giving me much of a trusting look right now."

Kevin drank a swig of water from his bottle again, then bowed his head.

"What? Are you having something with Kyle?" His heart dropped. His comment was uncalled for, but the question burst from him. He doubted Kevin was doing anything with Kyle. "Kevin?"

"I need a moment to process this, but no, I'm not doing anything with Kyle." Kevin sat on the arm of the sofa. "Here's the thing. I do trust you. I'm sure you're going to see him to get your stuff and that'll be the end of it."

"But?"

"It doesn't exactly make me want to do handsprings," Kevin said. "You must've known about this meeting before today and yet you just now told me. It doesn't inspire confidence."

"I was afraid you'd be upset."

"I am."

"Kevin." *Fuck, fuck, fuck.*

"I'm upset because I wish you'd have told me when you first decided. I'm not jealous of him and I know you're not going to fuck him, but I was hurt by my ex not telling me the truth."

"I wanted to," Shaun said. He brushed an errant lock of Kevin's hair off his brow. "It didn't feel right to tell you in a wild moment. I didn't want to ruin things."

"I know." Kevin stood, then embraced Shaun. "And now I know." He brushed his nose along Shaun's. "We'll get through this."

"I love you, Kev, and I don't want to hurt you." *Never.*

"I know."

"I'm sorry."

"I know." Kevin tipped his head to meet Shaun's gaze. "It'll be okay. Promise. I'm not going anywhere — except to work — and I'll have my phone with me tonight if you need me."

"Don't get into trouble."

"I won't."

He held Kevin tight. He knew he'd made the right choice when he'd met him. He'd found his guy. "Want to shower with me?"

"I would if I didn't need to get moving. I spent too long here already, but I'm glad I did. I wanted this worked out." Kevin kissed him. "I regret nothing."

"Where are you going?" Shaun asked. "The game isn't until one, right?"

"As the head of concessions, I'm going over the figures with Mr. Vale. Sales are up since the promotions started and the workforce is happier," Kevin said. "He wanted to meet to discuss strategies for next season."

"Does this mean you might not be spending so much time working the counter?" And more time watching the game, preferably with him.

"If I play my cards right." Kevin kissed him again. "If revenue stays up, we can hire more people. It seems to be so far and Mr. Vale is tossing around ideas for using the stadium in the off-season. Who knows? I might get to stay out from behind the counter for good."

"I hope so."

"Me, too." Kevin hesitated another moment. "Get moving. You don't want to be late to get those pictures back."

"No, I don't."

"I can't make you dinner if you're not home." Kevin grinned. "To celebrate."

He wasn't sure what they were celebrating and didn't care. "I'm in and I will hurry as much as legally possible."

"See you tonight." Kevin grabbed his shirt, water bottle and keys. "You can do this."

"Love you." Shaun wanted to ignore everything else in his day and be with Kevin. God, he was lucky to have such an understanding man in his life.

Chapter Nine

Once Kevin left, Shaun showered and shaved. He dressed in khakis and a short-sleeve button-down. His outfit wasn't haute couture, but who needed to be super fashionable? Not him. He wasn't going to meet Jonah to impress him.

He ate a granola bar and filled his water bottle, then headed to work. Since Monday, he hadn't heard anything on three of the houses he'd inquired about and wondered if they'd already sold. The first two houses had been a bust—too small, and he'd never afford the renovations on his salary. He spent his shift working on the newest ads and rearranging the Sunday page to accommodate the garage sale listings.

Remy caught up with him in the hallway. "I wanted to tell you I'm pleased with your work and I love the stories about the pets. You're making them so adorable I want to adopt them all. Who is next week's feature?"

"I'm not sure. The one we had lined up was adopted, so we'll have to pick another tomorrow," Shaun said.

"I'm glad. I'd rather have to keep looking for new ones

than have a poor critter linger there." He still wanted to adopt his own cat, too.

"I know." Remy stopped him. "I had a strange email today and wanted to discuss something with you." He gestured to Shaun's office.

"Sure." He had no idea what Remy might have been emailed about. He shut the door. "What's up?"

"Did you tell anyone you needed an assistant?" Remy asked.

Shaun chuckled, then sobered. "No, why?"

"A man emailed me saying you'd requested an assistant—him—and would I consider this person for the job," Remy said. "I give him props for having the balls to ask for the job, but it sounds so strange. You didn't say anything, even something in a stray comment, did you? It didn't sound like something you'd do, but I have to ask."

"I haven't asked for an assistant or mentioned it to someone in passing. I appreciate you being thorough and asking, but it wasn't me." Shaun folded his arms. "I haven't met enough people socially that aren't with the paper to have such a conversation."

"I suspected as much."

"This person used my name?"

"They did."

"May I ask who it was?" *Who would want to use my name for a reference?*

"Kyle Beglin."

Shaun sank onto his chair. "He works for the ballclub. I thought he did their promo."

"He did—until he was fired." Remy sat across from him. "I did some checking. Not only was Mr. Beglin fired, but escorted out of the building. I guess he'd been mishandling team funds. He stole money from the promotions department, paid it back, and the team isn't planning to use legal methods to handle it—as long as he never returns to the premises. It's a mess."

"So he needs another job." Shaun leaned back in his chair. "My assistant—if there was such a thing—wouldn't pay much. I'm guessing he hadn't thought of that."

"But it's a job," Remy said. "I suspect once people see why he was terminated, they'll be less likely to hire him, which is why he tried for this before the news came out all over town."

"But why use my name? I don't even like him."

"Because of Kevin?"

"Among other things. I met Kyle at the newspaper day we held at the stadium. He got right in my face, told me we'd be good together and was too pushy. That's what turned me off. The connection to Kevin was an extra annoyance," Shaun said. "He was rude to Kevin, too. I don't want to work with that kind of person."

"I can see where it might be difficult."

Shaun stared at Remy. "I have no idea why he'd want to work here, but my professional opinion is we don't need the help. We're good the way we are."

"Very well. I'll respond to his email with a polite no—which I'd planned on giving him from the beginning." Remy stood. "You didn't strike me as the name-dropper type."

"I'm not."

Remy shrugged. "There's using someone's name to get a story, then there's name-dropping to get ahead. This was to cover his ass and get out of trouble. I don't want that headache. Thanks."

"Sure." This time Shaun laughed, but to hide his annoyance. He waited until Remy left, then checked his email.

A message from Kyle popped into his inbox.

Dear Mr. Fallows,

My name is Kyle Beglin. I'm sure you remember me from the newspaper part and my work with the Cedarwood Wildcats baseball team. We spoke at length about my joining the Tribune as your assistant and I'd like to take you up on your offer. I've listed my qualifications on my resume and have been given high praise by Mr. Nicholas. I hope you're still interested in giving me the position. I won't let you down.

Respectfully yours,
Kyle Beglin

That *shit*. He read the email twice more to be sure he'd really seen it. Ballsy was right. He'd made up a job position. Kevin had said Kyle could manipulate and he wasn't wrong.

Shaun forwarded the email to Remy with the note, *I never offered him a job.*

He logged out of his email, then called the animal shelter to confirm his appointment the next day with Stone McCartney.

At three, he packed up his things and locked his office. Before he drove to the truck stop, he needed to see Kevin. He left the newspaper building and drove over to the stadium. He parked, bought a ticket and went straight to Kevin's concession stand. There weren't many people in line. *Good.* Maybe he'd get a chance to talk to his boyfriend and boost his spirits.

When it was his turn, he darted over to Nedra. "Hi. I'd like a soda and Kevin."

"He's in his office," she said. "Three bucks for the drink and I'll get him." She grinned. "You know, I haven't seen him this happy in a long time. I don't know what you're doing, but keep it up."

He counted the bills and waited for her to return. Nedra reappeared a moment later with Kevin. She handed over the soda. "One beverage and one Kevin, over there."

Kevin half-smiled. "I didn't think you'd come up here."

"Can you come out for five minutes?" Shaun asked. He held tight to the paper cup.

"Sure." Kevin left the counter and appeared at the side door. "What's wrong?"

"Nothing." Shaun paused. "No, it's not nothing." He lowered his voice and inched closer to Kevin.

"We can't make out here," Kevin joked. "Not that I'd be upset if we did." His smile faded. "Shaun?"

"Kyle contacted the paper."

"About what?"

"In not so many words, he asked for a job. He said I encouraged him. Kevin, he got fired from his position here and tried to use me to gain a position at the *Tribune*."

"Wow." Kevin grabbed Shaun's sleeve. "You're serious?"

"It won't work because Remy's on to him, but still. Just watch your back," Shaun said. "I don't trust him."

Kevin nodded. "I will. You be careful, too." He let go and slid his fingers down Shaun's arm. "Thanks for telling me."

"After the day I've had—and I haven't seen Jonah yet—I'm worried. It's like every clusterfuck has come together and it's getting me in the ass," Shaun said.

"It'll be okay." Kevin tugged him closer. "You're my guy. Kyle can't touch us and neither can Jonah. I'm not going anywhere and it sounds like Remy has your back, too."

He nodded and embraced the reassurances from Kevin. "Sorry, I'm dramatic."

"It's okay. Dramatic means you're human." Kevin swatted him on the ass. "Get done. I'm seriously fixing dinner tonight, so don't be late."

"I won't." Shaun sighed. If Kevin wasn't worried, then he wasn't either. "See you. I'll call when I'm on my way."

"Sounds good." Kevin kissed him on the cheek. "You got this."

"I do, because I have you." Shaun left the ballpark and headed out to his car. He tucked the drink into the cupholder then headed down to Ashland. The drive afforded him time to think about the other house listings he'd seen and what he wanted in a home. He still preferred the extra bedrooms and the yard, but he might be able to negotiate on the larger garage or the privacy fences. Maybe if he and Kevin worked together on the renovations, they'd be able to afford to upgrade.

Maybe.

Once he reached Ashland, he pulled into the parking lot of the truck stop. He parked. He'd forgotten how busy the place could be—so much action and so many people. This wasn't the type of establishment he usually frequented—it was too far out of the way. But the truck stop was public enough for a meeting with Jonah.

He ventured inside and swept his gaze over the mix of people at the various tables. Jonah stood next to one of the tables and waved his arm.

Shaun fortified himself. *Face him, get the pictures and get moving.*

"Shaun." Jonah threw his arms around Shaun. "You made it."

"I did." He gave his ex-boyfriend a limp hug in return. "How was the drive?"

"Good. Columbus is really happening." Jonah gestured to the empty chair. "Sit. I'll get coffees. Still plain with two creamers?"

"Yeah." Among other drinks. He'd evolved in his coffee selections.

Jonah returned a moment later with two cups. "So. You look good. Are you happy? Here."

"Thank you." He accepted one of the coffees.

"Welcome. You're still thin, but it looks like you put on muscle." Jonah sat across from him. "You look happy."

"I'm running more."

"Good for you," Jonah said. "I remember when I'd watch you run the races. It was so cool to see you at the end. You made those races look effortless."

"It wasn't." The last he knew, Jonah hated going to the competitions and dealing with the sweaty people. He'd remind Shaun he was bored and hated the inaction while he waited for Shaun to finish.

"You looked great in those little shorts, too." Jonah laughed and held up his paper cup. "To the races."

"Sure." *What an odd toast.* He slid his gaze over Jonah. He used to think Jonah was so polished. Jonah always had his glossy black hair slicked perfectly back and his dark eyes were always vibrant. He never had a hair out of place or five-o'clock shadow. So pressed and maintained. But now? He seemed almost too perfect. Was he wearing mascara? He'd darkened the bit of gray he'd had at his temples. Did it matter? Jonah was and always had been too much upkeep and drama for him. Shaun liked Kevin's easy style—not trying to be anyone but himself.

"You're staring at me." Jonah raked his fingers through his hair. "Am I okay?"

"You're fine. Stop worrying."

"I hate when there's no order." Jonah fiddled with his hair again. "Better?"

"It's good." He'd learned a long time ago that it was better to placate Jonah than to argue. "Do you have the photos?"

"Yes." Jonah fished around in his sport coat, then withdrew an envelope. "Here."

"Thanks." Shaun tamped down his surprise. Jonah had forked over something. He flipped through the images in the envelope. Three of the pictures were of his mother alone, two were from his parents' wedding day, two were of his father in a tuxedo and a dozen or so of the images were of Shaun and Jonah together. "What's this?"

"Us. Those are your copies." Jonah pointed to one of the images. "Your mom looks so young."

"She was nineteen when they married." He shuffled back to the pictures of him and Jonah. "No, these."

"You don't want them?" Jonah reached for the envelope.

"That's not it." He held firm to the photographs. "I meant, why did you print pictures of us together? We're not a couple."

"Your mom's dress is so retro. I love it. She looked wonderful," Jonah said, ignoring Shaun's questions.

"She did." He hated when Jonah declined to answer.

"I always thought you looked like our father."

"Good, since I'm his kid." He didn't like the strange feeling between him and Jonah. They were being nice and pleasant to each other and it was good to have conversation without arguing. Jonah sort of reminded him of an old sweater — comfortable and stable. But this was strange, too. Jonah, as a sweater, didn't fit quite right.

Jonah reached across the table and grasped Shaun's fingers. "I wanted you to remember the good times. We had ten years together and did so much. You can't ignore it."

The warning bells went off in Shaun's mind. He recoiled and kept the photos under his palm. "No. I'm with someone." The good-ish feelings melted in an instant.

"So am I."

"What?" He tucked the envelope into the breast pocket of his shirt. "Why would you do that to him?"

"Because you're my soulmate." Jonah reached across the table again. "We should be together."

"No, we shouldn't." He pushed away from the table and stood. His stomach soured. He wasn't in the mood for truck stop coffee or Jonah's bullshit.

"You're my number one," Jonah said.

"You're just trying to use me, and you're lying, like you always do. This is your fucked-up way of convincing me to come back, and it's not working." Shaun shook his head. "I can't be with you because it's not right and I'm not interested. We split and I'm with someone." He pushed his chair in. "Were there any other pictures?"

"I'll keep looking," Jonah said. "Don't go. Don't leave this way."

Shaun withdrew his business card from his wallet. "If you find any other photos, send them here."

"The *Tribune*? *This* is your big time?" Jonah said and snorted. "What kind of backwoods paper is this? Is it even real?"

"I'm just a guy and this is the town paper. I do my job and I'm paid well for it." He wasn't in the mood for games. He had what he needed and it was time to go. Kevin had been brave about the situation, but Shaun had hurt his boyfriend and he refused to waste any more time.

"So that's it?" Jonah followed him out of the building. "Ten years and this is all we are?"

"Yes." He hated public arguments.

"I thought you loved me."

Shaun paused and lowered his voice. "I did. I gave you my heart and you crushed it when you cheated on me with Nick, Steven, Drake, the other Jean, Geno...the list is too long to remember them all. You wanted freedom and I had the misguided idea you'd change. Nope. I grew up and you can't. Accept it and that I'm not yours. Thanks for the photographs."

"You're leaving? Like that? I cleared my evening for you," Jonah said. "You owe me."

"I'm sure you'll find someone to fill the time. You always do." He headed over to his car. "Goodbye, Jonah." He slid behind the wheel of his vehicle and locked the doors. His love for Jonah had died, never to be rekindled, now that he had closure.

Shaun drove home. The tension in his shoulders remained, but he could handle it because he was going to Kevin's apartment, to his man.

* * * *

Kevin finished his paperwork for the night and headed to Mr. Vale's office. He wanted a jump on his day off and the only way that would happen was if he hand-delivered the figures. He'd never been to the main offices before and knocked on Mr. Vale's door. He expected a secretary outside, but the desk was empty.

"Come. The door's open," Mr. Vale called.

Kevin ventured into the office. Mr. Vale sat behind his desk and looked up. "Ah, Mr. Keiser. Well? How are our numbers? The lines looked good."

"Even with the win, we did very well. People tend to buy more food when we're losing—to drown out their sorrows, I'm told." He offered up the piece of paper. "I've emailed the figures to you as well, but here are the totals. I've got more breakdowns in the email."

"Good." Mr. Vale nodded. "I knew you'd be an asset." He trailed his finger over the lines on the paper and didn't look up. "Got any plans for your day off?"

"I do, but it depends on what you say," Kevin said.

"Oh?" This time, Mr. Vale looked at him. "How so?"

"Mr. Mulhenney expected forty-hour weeks even when we didn't have games. Cleaning, sanitizing, paperwork, whatever. He wanted us here no matter what and I'd like to enjoy my break. It's up to your rules, but that's my thought."

"You went above and beyond today, like everyone else. The facility is closed tomorrow, save for the custodial staff, so enjoy your day off," Mr. Vale said. "You don't need to be here."

"Thank you." He sighed with relief. *A day off without strings. Nice.*

"Oh, I've heard you're friends with Kyle Beglin," Mr. Vale said. "Are you?"

"I was."

"Were you close?"

"We were for a time, but not any longer."

"Ah." Mr. Vale placed the paperwork aside on his desk. "So you know, since it'll be going around the building in the gossip, I fired him. He wasn't spending the promotional money on the team, but rather on himself. We ran the numbers and they weren't adding up—turns out he'd claimed his clothing and food expenses as team promotion. That's not how I work here." He shook his head. "When questioned, he had the audacity to say you'd encouraged him to mishandle the funds. You'd sullied his reputation."

Oh God. "I did? How?" He'd barely talked to Kyle once they split.

"That doesn't matter. I asked everyone I could think of to give me their thought on the situation and no one had an unkind word to say about you. No one mentioned a thing to back up Mr. Beglin's story."

"Good?" He wasn't sure what to say.

"I'm told you have a degree in advertising. Have you thought about applying for the promotional job?" Mr. Vale asked. "Would you be happier in promotion?"

"I like working in the concessions and food services aspect here at the stadium. My thoughts on promotions would be better there, than at a desk." Kevin laced his fingers together. "I'm not good at talking to the public unless I'm selling food. Sorry."

"Fair enough and understood. How about Mr. Shaun Fallows?" Mr. Vale asked. "I'm told he might be good in that position. Is he looking for a new job?"

"I don't think so. He's working for the *Tribune* and we've worked with him on special sections for the paper. We've got one of their four-page inserts free at all the entrances," Kevin said. "I doubt he's looking for a new job."

"Think you could convince him to try us?"

"I can't speak for him and you'd have to ask, but I know he's happy at the *Tribune*."

"Fair enough." Mr. Vale stood. "Enjoy your evening and tomorrow off. You deserve it. I've sent a plan for the rest of the season to you and we'll have a meeting Friday about off-season promotions. I'm thinking about doing something with movie nights or a holiday lights family walk-through. We've got the tarps to cover the field, so nothing will get ruined, but we've got to use the park for something outside the games."

"I'm sure you'll think of something, but the lights thing sounds good." Kevin nodded. "Maybe work it with the town to have a big festival of lights and a tour around town? They haven't done that in years. Remember?"

"I do." Mr. Vale's eyes lit up. "That is a great idea. Thank you."

"Welcome. See you Friday." Kevin left the office. He had nothing to do for a whole day. No surprise demands for him to come in, no last-minute clean-ups...he could veg out or get a long run in. Could spend time with Shaun, too. *Holy shit.* They could look at houses together, too.

The thought warmed his heart.

If someone had asked him a year ago if he'd be this happy, he would've laughed.

He left the facility and climbed behind the wheel of his car, then drove home. He wasn't sure what to make for Shaun. He wasn't the greatest cook—hot dogs and nachos weren't exactly grand fare. Did he have much in the fridge? *Cat food...* He parked in his spot at the apartment and left the vehicle.

"Hi, stranger." Shaun walked up to him. "Good game?"

"Very." He locked his car. "You're here. Rough meeting?"

"Very."

"What happened?" He wanted to kiss Shaun, but was unsure if it was the right move.

"I'll tell you upstairs while we wait for the pizza to arrive." Shaun threaded his arm around Kevin's and started walking. "I know you said you'd cook, but we're both tired and pizza is faster, plus, there's no clean-up. Well, not much," he said. "I ordered when I saw your car pull in."

"I suppose you're right, and it saves me from trying to figure out what to feed you—since I hadn't thought this through very well." He kissed Shaun. "I'm glad you're here." His boyfriend buoyed him.

"There we go. I'm glad to be here." He headed into the apartment building with Kevin. "I'm beat."

"I'll bet, but I'm tired, too."

Shaun led the way up the stairs. "They won, though. I saw the score. It was a tight game."

Kevin unlocked the apartment door and as he stepped inside, he hooked his keys on the rack. Leo trotted up to him and he scooped the cat into his arms. "Hi, baby. I know I was gone all day." He met Shaun's gaze. "Sorry. This is our usual routine when I come home."

"You won't get an argument from me." Shaun checked his phone, then closed the door. "The pizza is still baking. Why don't you shower? It won't be here for at least another twenty minutes."

"I'd rather you come with me." He still held the cat, but spoke to Shaun. "I doubt we'll have enough time." He plopped Leo onto his cat tree. "How about after?"

"Yes." Shaun dropped his phone onto the sofa and crossed the room. He caught Kevin in his embrace and kissed him. The deep, passionate, consuming kiss warmed Kevin all over.

Kevin shoved his hand beneath Shaun's shirt, needing to touch his lover's skin. He craved this man.

Shaun broke the kiss first. "Needed that."

"So did I." He'd like more. "You don't have to stop."

"Let me tell you about my day first. I need to get this out." Shaun let go and threaded his fingers together, propping his hands on the back of his head. "I met with Jonah."

Kevin sat on the arm of the sofa. "You said you would." When Leo hopped off the cat tree and joined him on the couch, Kevin cuddled the cat on his lap.

"I met with him and he gave me these." Shaun withdrew an envelope. "Pictures. Some are of Mom, some of Dad, some of them together and mostly Jonah and me."

I should've guessed.

"I didn't want those, but he said I needed reminders of what I've been through. Jesus Christ. I'm over forty. I don't need to look back," Shaun said. "I'm in my prime."

"You are." He didn't say more. This was Shaun's time to vent.

Shaun faced him. "For a split second, I remembered why I thought I loved him. The old feelings rushed in and it was almost like old times, but then he said something that brought me right back to now. He asked me to hook up with him and I said no. I told him I was with someone and he replied that he's with someone, too. He's with someone and willing to ignore that person for a moment's pleasure. I can't do that. I won't, and the idea that he could…it churned my stomach. Kev, he did that all along."

Kevin continued to pet Leo. "I wouldn't cheat on you, either."

"I know." Shaun paced the length of the room. "That moment encapsulated the relationship. He wanted me to go against my principles for him. Always for him."

"But you didn't."

"No." Shaun unwound his hands and cupped Kevin's jaw. "When I look into your eyes, I see my future. I see us and Leo and even another cat or two in our own little house. I see us growing old together and that's what I want. I wasn't lying when I said I love you. I do."

"I know, and I never doubted you." He kissed the inside of Shaun's wrist. "Not for a second."

"You're just freaked out. So am I. Between Kyle trying to use me to get a job, Jonah acting like he knows what's best for me and the worry in your eyes when I told you I love you, it all nearly killed me."

"I care about you, Shaun, but I'm scared. If I go too fast and tell you how I feel, I'm scared it'll fall apart."

"It won't." Shaun let go and knelt in front of him. "You've got me."

"I do?"

"All of me. Do I have all of you?"

The couch vibrated, interrupting the moment. Kevin sighed. "I'm guessing that means the pizza is done and they're downstairs."

Shaun shrugged. "It happens." He stood. "Are you happy it saved you from having to answer?"

"No." He left his seat and tucked Leo under his arm. "You have all of me, too."

"Kevin?"

"There's no one else I want in my life and bed. Just you."

"Truth?" Shaun petted Leo's head and threaded his free arm around Kevin. "Don't say what you're not feeling."

He kissed Shaun, careful not to squish Leo between them. "I've fallen hard for you. It's love—even if I'm scared to say those three words. You're the one in my heart. No one else. Just you." He refused to pour his heart out under duress, but Shaun needed reassurance.

"I can accept that." Shaun brushed his nose along Kevin's. "Let me get dinner."

"I'll be here with Leo." Kevin let go and waited for Shaun to leave before he exhaled. The fear of admitting he loved Shaun overwhelmed him. He knew his heart. He did love Shaun. But he'd been hurt before and didn't want to go through the pain. Not a second time. Shaun had the power to destroy him, and maybe that was the reason he feared telling Shaun he loved him. He worried Shaun would tear his heart into pieces. *God.* He'd never cared about anyone in the way he did with Shaun.

The door opened and Shaun strode into the apartment with the pizza box. "It's definitely hot." He closed the door, then carried the box to the counter. "At least we know it's fresh."

"True." He waited until Shaun put the keys down and took his shoes off, then Kevin grasped Shaun's hand. "Just a minute."

"Kevin?" Shaun frowned. "You're pale."

He needed to stop being scared. "I've never been in over my head before — not like I am with you. I've never cared about someone so much. I'm afraid to tell you how I feel because I don't want to get hurt. I won't be the same if you go. You've changed me. I'm happier and more confident than ever, because of you. Do I love you? Yes. Shaun, I love you."

Shaun's lips parted and he said nothing. Kevin splayed his hand over Shaun's heart. He'd finally rendered Shaun speechless. Shaun threaded his arms around Kevin.

"I love you, too." Shaun kissed Kevin hard. "So much."

The tension he'd carried since he'd split from Kyle finally melted away. He didn't have to be anyone but himself. He embraced the love in his heart and passion for Shaun. "Now we can celebrate."

"Yes." Shaun laughed. "Completely." He held Kevin tight. "You had me worried. Thought you'd dump me or something."

"Nah. I'm like that tattoo on your shoulder. I'm here and not going anytime soon," Kevin said. "I'm even looking forward to looking at houses with you."

"You are?"

"Sure." He nodded to the pizza. "We should eat before our super-hot pizza gets cold."

Kevin opened the pizza box while Shaun got out plates. He loved the homey feel. They were good together. Shaun was the sauce to his cheese.

"You're grinning." Shaun heaped two slices of pizza onto his plate. "What are you thinking about?"

"You. Me." He added a slice to his plate and followed Shaun to the couch. He sat with his boyfriend and turned on music. "I'm thinking about how easy this is. How I like the way we fit together."

Shaun sat beside him. "We do." He leaned into Kevin. "This is nice." He rested his head on Kevin's shoulder.

Kevin sighed and ate. This was what he wanted — the guy, the cat, the happy home. His life had leveled out. He listened to the music and enjoyed dinner with Shaun. Even Leo seemed to be happy with the situation.

"Who are we listening to? I chose the station, but I have no idea what this piece is that's playing," Kevin said. "I can't tell them apart."

"It's Rachmaninoff." Shaun chuckled. "I'll give you a crash course one of these days."

"Fair enough."

Shaun finished his first slice, then sat up. "Shit. I didn't get anything to drink."

"We're running in the morning. Water will be fine." He didn't need something fancy. "It's okay."

"Want more while I'm up?" Shaun asked.

"I'm good." He pushed his plate onto the coffee table. His thoughts were too focused on Shaun. "Feel better?"

"I do." Shaun returned with two glasses and sat with Kevin again. "I'm here with you, which is the best place." He kissed Kevin's shoulder. "You ground me."

Kevin forgot about his drink and Shaun's plate with a fresh slice of pizza, in favor of Shaun. He kissed him, needing Shaun to get closer.

Shaun brushed his nose along Kevin's jaw. He grasped Kevin's hand. "Come on." He tugged Kevin to his feet and led him into the bathroom.

Kevin didn't argue. He followed Shaun into the room. He had no words. He kissed him as Shaun opened the top of Kevin's polo shirt. A groan erupted in his throat as Shaun tugged the garment over his head.

Shaun grazed his hands over Kevin's chest. He licked and nipped at Kevin's mouth before swiping his tongue along Kevin's teeth.

Kevin groaned and opened to him. He breathed in the scent of Shaun's cologne, tasted the spice of the pizza on his kiss, and held tight to his lover. The power and devotion in Shaun's grasp blew his mind.

Shaun turned the water on in the shower. He shoved his hands down the back of Kevin's pants, massaging his ass.

"Shaun." Kevin whimpered. The pressure on his dick sent a shiver down his spine. He fumbled with Shaun's shorts, opening his fly. He needed to touch Shaun's dick. Warmth flooded his body and craving filled his veins.

Shaun withdrew his hands and unbuttoned Kevin's pants. He used no finesse as he pushed the denim down. Kevin's boxers ended up around his ankles. Shaun's gaze heated. "Get in the shower."

Kevin could do nothing but comply. He kicked out of the clothing, then removed his socks before climbing into the shower. The water stung his body, so hot and prickly. The steam billowed around him. He rested his head against the wall. His life had changed so much once he'd met Shaun, but in good ways. He'd opened up more and embraced what he wanted. He wasn't afraid of getting hurt or that Shaun might leave eventually, but not scared of Shaun or his own feelings. Now he just had to say the words.

Shaun joined him in the shower and caressed Kevin's chest. "You're still so tense." He nibbled Kevin's shoulder. He trailed his hands down Kevin's abs then to his groin. He didn't touch Kevin's dick and instead toyed with the hairs at the base of his erection.

The gentle caress scrambled Kevin's brain. Water sluiced down his face and stuck to his lashes. Heat infused his body.

Shaun angled him enough to face him and resumed stroking Kevin's pubic hair. "Let go, babe. Let your mind wander and enjoy this."

He gazed into Shaun's eyes. He'd never seen anything as sexy as his lover wet. Shaun's skin shimmered. A slight smile curled on his lips as he continued to stroke Kevin.

"You carry so much stress." He slid one arm around Kevin and curled his free hand around Kevin's dick. "You work so hard to keep yourself in line. You want to make everyone happy while forgetting yourself."

A groan vibrated in his throat. The stroking was so rhythmic and soothing. Kevin rocked into Shaun's fingers.

"You don't have to be strong with me all the time. You can crumble." Shaun brushed his lips against Kevin's cheek. "Come apart. I'm right here with you and I won't let you be destroyed."

Kevin threaded both arms around Shaun. Something shattered in him. It splintered, broke...changed him. No one ever spoke to him like this or cared this much. He rocked his groin into Shaun's hand, bumping against his boyfriend's shaft.

Shaun opened his hand and collected his cock against Kevin's, stroking them together.

Kevin tensed. His synapses misfired. His balls were heavy and need nearly consumed him. Shaun had the magic touch. "Shaun."

Shaun kissed him hard and sucked on Kevin's tongue. He stole Kevin's breath.

Kevin forgot all about the water and ignored the world. All that mattered was Shaun.

Shaun bit Kevin's chin. "Want to come?"

He hadn't realized how close he was to falling apart until Shaun said those words. He pushed into Shaun's hand, loving the feel of dick on dick. He dug his fingers into Shaun's side, holding on for dear life. He had no thoughts, no worries. Shaun consumed him. His knees weakened as he pistoned into Shaun's hand. He panted and the sound of his growl was loud in his ears.

"Do it," Shaun said. He stroked faster. "Come for me. Gets me hot seeing you lose control."

Kevin shuddered. His body tensed as his resistance shattered. He embraced the orgasm. "Fuck." He jammed his cock into Shaun's hand and came. A ribbon of cum landed on the floor of the shower stall. His head swam. He wobbled into Shaun and panted again.

"Beautiful," Shaun murmured. "Love it."

Kevin sagged into his boyfriend's arms. Every inch of his body tingled.

"You're sexy when you come," Shaun said. He stroked Kevin's chest. "I want to be inside you."

Kevin groaned. "Want you inside me." He managed to turn around. He stuck his ass out at Shaun and flattened his cheek to the wall. "Do it."

"Yeah." Shaun caressed Kevin's asshole. He rocked against Kevin, sliding his dick along the crack of Kevin's ass. He dribbled shower gel down Kevin's back.

A fresh wave of heat engulfed him. Kevin embraced the relaxation now. He flattened his hands on the tiles. "Shaun."

"Right here." He ground against Kevin, not penetrating him.

The anticipation ratcheted up Kevin's need. He panted and arched into Shaun.

Shaun added more slippery shower gel along Kevin's back until the gel covered Kevin's asshole. Shaun eased one digit into Kevin. "Breathe, baby."

Kevin wanted to. He'd been relaxed by Shaun, but his excitement returned to a fever pitch. His legs trembled.

Shaun moved his finger in and out of Kevin while he raked his teeth along the back of Kevin's neck. "Want me?"

"Yes." He loved how Shaun pushed and teased him. Shaun knew how much Kevin wanted him. "Please?" He rocked into Shaun's finger. "Want more of you in me."

"Damn." Shaun pumped his finger faster then withdrew. He prodded Kevin's hole with the blunt head of his erection. "Breathe for me."

Kevin bore down as Shaun pushed inside him. The fit and oneness were too much to handle. Kevin's thoughts scrambled again. He clawed at the tiles.

"Fits me perfectly." Shaun whimpered against Kevin's neck. "I want to stay here forever."

He'd be okay with that. Kevin wriggled his hips, nudging Shaun's cock against his prostate. "Yes."

"You make me so hot." Shaun grasped Kevin's hips. "Need you." He eased most of the way out before pushing deep again, building into a steady rhythm.

Skin on skin, soul to soul. Kevin backed against him. "More."

The one-word command must've been more than enough for Shaun. He increased the speed of his thrusts and mashed Kevin into the wall.

Christ, this is hot. Kevin met him thrust for thrust, needing him deep inside. He lost himself in the divine feeling of being loved. Shaun loved him all the way, no kidding. As realization washed over him, the second orgasm hit. He'd never had so many multiple climaxes, but Shaun did that to him. He cried out and flexed around Shaun.

"God. Squeezing me." Shaun groaned. "I won't last." His thrusts increased in ferocity. "Fuck."

"Let go," Kevin managed. "Do it." He'd echoed Shaun's words and didn't care. His own resistance shattered again. He tensed, then relaxed. He hadn't even touched his dick, yet everything within him mellowed as he basked in the post-orgasmic glow.

"Yes." Shaun pounded in him, then growled. He surged into Kevin and his cock twitched. Shaun slid his arms around Kevin and collapsed on him. His breath tickled against Kevin's ear.

Instead of speaking, Kevin lingered in the sublime thrill of being with his lover. He'd found his person. Hell, he'd been changed when he'd met Shaun, and even more now. He'd let his guard down without getting hurt. He was treasured and loved. He knew his heart, too. He loved Shaun more than anything.

Water sluiced over his body as Shaun clung to him. His life was different. He couldn't see his existence without Shaun. His loneliness was no more and he knew what he wanted.

Shaun pulled out and eased away from Kevin. "You fry my brain every time."

Kevin faced Shaun and yanked him close. "I love you, Shaun." His world righted and his heart was happy. "So much." He had no regrets and didn't even worry about how Shaun would react. He knew.

"I love you, too." Shaun kissed him. "We should make the coffee table our spot and this shower our place. I never want to leave it."

"Even if we get pruney?" Kevin asked.

"You mean *when*?"

"That, too," Kevin said. "Whenever I'm with you, I'm home."

"You're my home, too." Shaun held him. "Be we should get cleaned up before the water gets cold."

"Good point." Kevin added soap to the washcloth. "We should clean up the rest of the pizza, too. I'll bet Leo is out there nibbling on the crust. It won't hurt him, but he shouldn't eat it." He slid his hands over Shaun, scrubbing his lover clean. "But for next time."

Shaun's eyes widened and he rinsed. "I'll take care of it." He ducked under the spray and rinsed before he left the stall. "Leo?"

Kevin chuckled, then ducked under the spray. The last of the hot water slid down his back. He washed himself, first his body then hair. His thoughts turned to Shaun. He'd finally found a guy who cared about Leo as much as he did. Shaun was the first guy to absolutely love him and Leo like a package deal. He had everything he'd ever wanted in Shaun with no regrets.

Shaun was his other half.

He turned the water off, then stepped out of the stall and grabbed a towel. He dried himself and listened for Shaun. "Everything okay?" He strode out of the bathroom and ventured into the bedroom.

Shaun stood in the middle of the room, naked. "I got the pizza picked up and the glasses are in the sink. Leo seemed no worse for wear."

As if on cue, Leo hopped onto the bed, then sprawled out and cleaned himself.

"It would appear." Kevin ditched the towel in the bathroom, then slid between the sheets. "Come here. We've got the rest of our life to worry about Leo and be together. I want to hold you."

Shaun flipped the light switch and joined him in bed. "You had me at come here."

Kevin held his lover and snuggled in the sheets. He'd be happy as long as he had Shaun. His life was just as he'd always wanted — perfect.

Chapter Ten

A week and a half later, Kevin followed Shaun into the fourth house. If he'd have known house hunting would be so boring, he'd have stayed at the apartment. He hated traipsing through another person's house and finding the faults with it.

He stood in the living room of the blue house and admired the bland white walls. The room could use a bolder hue. He liked the view out of the bay window — sunny, but leafy and would be nice with a few plants or a cat tree. The neighborhood pleased him. He could run there and not have to worry about driving to the Metroparks.

Shaun and Tony, the realtor, ventured off, leaving Kevin to himself. Just as well. Kevin trailed his fingers over the woodwork. The plain paneling appealed to him as much as the wall of recessed bookshelves. He liked the cottage feel of the house, too. If he remembered right, the neighborhood had been constructed in the forties and the home certainly displayed the midcentury charm. The window seat in the front room would be a great place for Leo to sun himself. The carpet in the living room might need an upgrade, but that wasn't impossible.

He'd seen the back yard in the photos online, but wanted to view the space for himself. He made his way to the rear of the home and pushed open the French doors to the patio. The yard was bigger than the photographs displayed. The line of bushes and fencing was higher than he'd thought, too. Walled-in and private, just like he wanted.

Shaun's voice filtered to him as Shaun joined him on the patio. "Hey," Shaun said. "What do you think?"

"Read me off the stats again." Kevin sat on the half-wall lining three sides of the patio. "I like the back yard and the living room is great. The recessed shelves and window seat are wonderful. I'd change the carpet, but I don't remember if this house was supposed to have hardwood under the carpet. Probably not. Is this the one with the hidden hardwood floors? I can't remember, and the other houses all sort of looked the same."

"This one is four-fifty-two Hemlock. It's got four bedrooms and the two-car garage like we wanted." Shaun hesitated. "I wanted. The ranch style is nice because it's all one floor, and the basement is finished. I love the giant oak in the back yard, too." He folded his arms. "The community is quiet and the sidewalks look wide enough for runs."

"Agreed." Kevin wondered if Shaun realized he'd slipped and said 'we'. He must've, as he'd fixed his comment. "I like the dated look of the kitchen. The scalloped soffits are cute and we could refinish them or paint them down the road. It's certainly all original."

Shaun nodded. "The blue is fetching."

"What was the price on this one?"

"About twenty grand over my range." Shaun sighed. "Tony said the seller will drop the price, but even with a drop, I'll need help—either a roommate or partner."

Kevin crooked his brow. "So do you have a roommate in mind?"

Shaun paled. "Kev, I really want you to move in with me, but I can't force it. I don't want to put you in that position."

Kevin took the preapproval form from Shaun and checked over the potential payment if they bought the house just under the asking price. "I can help with this—but it'd be nice if we can talk them down a bit more." He needed to put down roots. "Why should we have two places when we only need one?"

"Kevin?"

He shrugged. "You love this house. It's available and mostly move-in ready. Everything is clicking into place and I think this is the cosmos telling us to do this."

"You want to live with me?"

"Do you want to live with me and Leo?" Kevin asked. "It's better than trying to steal moments together here and there." He stood next to Shaun and stared out at the back yard. "I can see that date we discussed, plus a lot more."

Shaun's eyes widened. "Kevin?"

"I want to do this. We can spend the rest of our lives here, making this house ours."

"Guys?" Tony joined them on the patio. "There's another couple wanting to look at the house, but they're not overly enthused. We can talk to the seller again and I'm thinking they'll come down a bit more in price.

They want to sell today if possible. The preapproval gives you the leg up. What do you think?"

"We'd like to make an offer," Kevin said. "What we're each paying in rent for our individual apartments is more than enough for a house payment."

"Shaun?" Tony fiddled with his phone. "If this is what you want to do, I'll contact their realtor."

"Yes." Shaun nodded. "That's what we want to do."

"I'll be right back." Tony grinned, then left them on the patio.

"He's intense." Shaun shrugged, then turned his attention to Kevin. "So we're doing this?"

"Seems like." He'd never been more sure of anything — except being with Shaun — in his life.

"Marry me." Shaun held Kevin's hands. "I mean it. Marry me. If we're going in this far, we should go all the way. I love you and I want this."

Kevin laughed. He should've seen this coming, and oddly enough, he wasn't shocked by Shaun's declaration. "Let's buy the house first, then we can get married in the back yard when we're ready."

"You're not saying no, are you?" Shaun grinned and held tighter to Kevin's fingers. "You do want to marry me."

"I do."

"You saw the vision of us having our wedding back here, didn't you?" Shaun asked. "You saw it."

"I did. A silly archway of flowers, us tying the knot under the oak tree and lights ringing the back yard." He'd seen a little bit more, but this was enough for now.

"Yes."

"We need to run that race first, and get this house bought," Kevin said. "Get through the summer and plan over Christmas."

"Will you marry me?" Shaun held Kevin's hand. "We're buying this house, merging our stuff and getting Leo a friend."

"Then we'll get married." Kevin kissed Shaun. "Here comes Tony."

Shaun threaded his arm around Kevin. "Well?"

"The seller has twenty-four hours to accept the sale and to go over the details, but I talked to their realtor and they're wanting to move things along, so you should hear tonight." Tony held out his hand. "Unless something goes sideways, you're about to be homeowners."

"We are?" Shaun sagged into Kevin. "For real?"

"For real." Tony opened his folder. "Let's go inside and talk through the details, but I'm expecting to hear from them within the hour."

Kevin squeezed Shaun's hand. "Perfect."

* * * *

Two months later

Kevin finished the last touches and arranged the blanket. The summer was over and fall breezes kissed the Cedarwood landscape. He checked the bucket and fiddled with the ice. He needed this moment to be exactly right. Sheet in place, strings of twinkle lights on the fence and in the oak tree, projector on the table, wine chilling…all he needed now was to retrieve the plate of cheese and fruit.

"Kev?" Shaun strode out to the patio. "Where are you?"

"Here." Kevin stood. "You're early." He hadn't expected to see Shaun for another fifteen minutes.

"I am." Shaun held up the newspaper. "You have to see this. Kyle's been arrested. We just printed the story today."

"What?" Kevin abandoned the blanket. "He has?"

"For embezzlement. I guess the money trail at the stadium was longer than once thought. He stole more than a hundred grand." Shaun pointed to the article in the paper. "Remy wrote it up himself."

A photo of Kyle in handcuffs graced the front page of the paper. "Holy shit," Kevin murmured.

"Yep. Sure looks like he's out of our hair for good," Shaun said. "And not a moment too soon."

"Nope." Kevin took the paper from him. "I don't want to talk about him any longer." He held Shaun's hands.

Shaun's lips parted and he said nothing.

Kevin led him out to the yard. The setting sun helped add an orange glow to the space and enhanced the twinkle lights. Kevin tapped his phone and started the projector.

"Kevin." Shaun let go and wandered along the fence. "Is this...?" He met Kevin's gaze. "You created our date."

"I said I saw more out here." He pointed to the oak tree. The lights cascaded from the lower branches of the tree. "Like fireflies."

"It's like magic." Shaun held out his hand. "You made our date."

"I did." Kevin nodded to the sheet screen. His heart hammered as he headed into the house long enough to retrieve the cheese and fruit plate. Popcorn just didn't pair well with wine. He returned to the yard and Shaun stood in front of the screen.

Kevin put the plate down and poured wine into two glasses. He handed one of the wineglasses to Shaun. "Like it?"

"You made a video of us." Shaun's voice cracked. "Did you make this in your sleep? I never saw you work on it."

"I have spare time—sometimes." He threaded his free arm around Shaun. "We took our broken pieces and put them together to form our perfect puzzle."

A tear slid down Shaun's cheek. "We did."

Kevin fortified himself and placed his glass on the lawn. He fished in his pocket for the jewelry box, then dropped to one knee in front of Shaun. "My heart belongs to you and now we have a chance together. You've asked me to marry you at least three times. Now it's my turn. I'm not afraid of how I feel and I want to have a life with you. It takes a strong man to handle me and my cat, but you managed to not only win me over, but you got Leo to like you, too. That's huge." He withdrew the ring. "Shaun Michael Fallows, will you marry me?" He held up the black stainless-steel ring.

Shaun sank to his knees, then embraced Kevin. "I never thought this day would come."

Kevin held on to the ring and stroked the back of Shaun's head. "I wanted to do it right."

"You did." Shaun brushed his nose along Kevin's and another tear slid down his cheek.

"So? Will you marry me?" Kevin asked.

"Yes." Shaun kissed him. "Yes, yes, yes."

Kevin slid the ring onto Shaun's finger. "You're my fiancé now."

"I love how that sounds and I love you." Shaun rested his forehead against Kevin's and sighed. "This is so much better than my blurted requests."

Kevin shrugged. "I've had a lot of time to think about this and plan things." He held Shaun's hand. "I love you, too." He patted Shaun's hip. "Join me on the blanket. I've got wine, cheese, fruit and I want to celebrate."

"You thought of everything." Shaun stood, then moved to the blanket. "You're such a romantic."

"I'm your romantic." After Kevin picked up his glass of wine, he settled on the blanket and offered Shaun the other glass. "To us."

"To our future." Shaun clinked glasses with him. "Will we be hyphenated? Or take each other's name together? Or pick one? I'm kind of liking Shaun Keiser."

"As long as I have your love, I don't care how we handle our last name." He reclined against Shaun and settled in to watch the short-form video of their life together. Things would be complicated and messy, but beautiful, too. Why? He and Shaun were a couple for life and they'd have issues, but they'd get through them. He'd found his heart because Shaun had decided to start over in Cedarwood.

Want to see more from this author?
Here's a taster for you to enjoy!

Sun, Sea and…:
Sun, Sea and Summer Songs
Megan Slayer

Excerpt

Blake Payton stared at the monitor in his trailer and sighed. He wanted a change in life. Doing the bit part in the movie, a corny movie at that, bored him to tears. He lived to make music, and his career had seen him flying up the charts with pop songs guaranteed to make people dance.

Except no one wanted to listen to his songs anymore. The public wanted to see him deliver craptacular lines and engage in slapstick comedy. He raked his fingers through his hair, not giving a shit that he'd have to visit the hair and makeup trailer to fix his coif. *Screw it.* He wasn't important in the film and he doubted they'd miss him if he left the set.

He picked up the hand mirror he used to practice expressions and stared at his reflection. He might only be twenty-eight, but in the music business, that was old. Lines formed at the corners of his eyes when he smiled and… Were those circles forming beneath? Sure, this was the look required for his role in the movie, but did it have to accentuate his problem areas? He needed to put on his armor of makeup to hide behind. When he stepped into character, no one could touch him. Being bare meant the public saw everything. *Not good.*

He wasn't fresh and new—he'd been around the block a few times and made nine albums. Sure, he still drew a crowd when he played live, but his promoters swore it was the movies that brought in more money.

He hadn't started playing music for the money. He did it for the fame and adulation and later the chicks—except girls didn't do it for him. For years, he'd thought he was doing something wrong when he went out with women. The charge wasn't there. The instant attraction. He'd told himself the right girl hadn't come along, but he knew better. He wasn't attracted to women. Men—slick, sophisticated men—were his drug.

He tossed the mirror onto the sofa and turned his attention back to the monitor. One condition of his doing the movie involved him being able to have a television and access to entertainment outside the set. He loved to view the music videos of his equals and get a grasp on the up-and-coming artists.

Why did everyone on the music feeds have to look the same? Where was the style? The panache? The fun?

The veejay came onto the screen. "Now here's an oldie but a goodie. It's racing up the digital charts and proving to be the song for this summer. It's *Summer Song* by Payday, featuring Jude Sanders."

Blake sat up straight and peered at the screen. *He* was Payday—the ridiculous name his promoter had sworn he needed to break into the business—and Jude... He hadn't seen his friend in three years. He and Jude had recorded *Summer Song* at the apex of their relationship. Jude had claimed it would be a good way to show the world how much they meant to each other. Looking at the video and listening to the words now,

Blake believed it. The way Jude gazed at him and how they touched during the tender moments made it crystal clear that Jude had loved him—at the time. Now? He doubted Jude would talk to him.

He missed Jude, the way Jude held him, the touch of his hand, his kiss and the soulful look in his eyes when they made love.

Christ. He'd never gotten over Jude.

Jude had moved on, though. He'd begged Blake to admit to the world he was gay because Jude wanted to take the relationship public. Instead of following his heart, Blake had cowered behind his Payday persona and listened to his promoters. No one wanted him to be gay. They wanted the image of a fun, free pop star.

If the veejay was telling the truth, the song he'd recorded with Jude would be played everywhere. He'd never get away from the memories of their love and breakup. At least not for the duration of the summer.

Fuck.

Kel Templeton, his promoter, sauntered into the trailer. "What are you watching?"

"Videos." He didn't bother to turn the monitor off. "Remember the song I did with Jude Sanders? Three years down the road, it's a hit. *Summer Song* is the defining song of this season—according to the charts. What do you think about that?" He'd known the song was a hit when they'd recorded it, but Kel and others had seen it as a liability.

"Gag. You know why that is?" Kel asked. "Because a few disc jockeys and their veejay friends worked with influencers and kids on the internet to promote it. They made it happen. Big deal."

"If the numbers are right, then it *is* a big deal and will be a good payday." He switched off the monitor.

"I could use the money and chance to get back to playing music instead of doing these lousy movies."

"You're doing the movie. Period. You don't need to record music any longer. You can do this and get more attention. Remember how you wanted to do that bio pic? The Rat Ragland film? If you keep doing these and show your range, you'll get that film." Kel folded his arms. "You do realize you get more eyeballs this way."

"Eyeballs don't help when I'm not getting paid for the work." He fiddled with the mirror again. The memory of his reflection came to mind. He'd been made up to look old, and the creases and dark circles did him no favors. He wanted to record again. He came alive in the studio and music flowed in his soul. Playing the movie star wasn't his thing, no matter how much he wanted to do the punk rocker's bio flick. He hated trying to remember his lines while being someone else. Being himself was hard enough. His fans expected Payday, the flamboyant pop star with no holds barred. They wanted spectacle and sass.

"You're getting paid." Kel swatted Blake's arm. "Grow up and stop getting pissed. It's crap."

"Why?" He watched Kel flip through the book on the counter. Blake doubted Kel read much of anything, especially not Shakespeare. He wouldn't know a rhyming couplet from expository writing. Kel tossed the book onto the couch and glared at Blake. His stare could bore holes through steel when he got angry. Kel liked to use his hands and his thundering voice to get his point across. Most of the time, the tactic worked and Blake benefitted, but sometimes Kel could be abrasive and cruel.

"You have the whole summer ahead of you, so stop thinking about the past and enjoy the sun. You're in California. There's sun, fun and chicks. Get laid and shut up." Kel shook his head. "Ever since Jude got into your brain and messed with you, you've been off your game."

No kidding. Jude had churned up the feelings Blake thought he'd buried. Then again, Blake hadn't come out to Kel, and Kel had no idea Blake wasn't attracted to women. *Christ.* His behavior and appearance, wearing makeup and the rainbow colors, should've clued Kel in by now. Every time he did a collaboration, he did it with camp and style. He preferred to sing with other men and be flamboyant.

"Let me find you a chick. We'll get you sexed up and you'll chill out." Kel nodded. "I'll be back."

Blake sighed as his promoter left. He didn't want to be with a woman, random or otherwise. Truth be told, he wanted to be with Jude. That wasn't going to happen now, and he'd have to listen to their song all summer as a reminder of what he'd given up.

His phone rang. He slapped at the table, using the vibrations to move the device within reach. When he checked the ID screen, his heart hammered. Bob Casey. The last time he'd heard from his friend and former publicist, he'd set up the initial meeting between Blake and Jude. *What does Bob want?* "Hi, Bob."

"Blake, the man of the summer," Bob said. "How are you? Should be flying high. Have you seen the charts? They've picked up *Summer Song* in the clubs and there's talk of making a dance move for it. Nuts, right?"

"Nuts." He needed to investigate the popularity of his song. "I've seen some of the charts, but I hadn't heard anything about the clubs." He reclined on the couch. "How have you been? Organizing up a storm?"

"Not quite a storm, but I have an idea. I can get you a stadium tour to promote your music if you're willing to go out with Jude. Does that sound good? Sound like something you'd be interested in doing? I've got the whole thing pretty much lined up."

Blake wobbled back onto his seat. Shock washed over him. *Bob can't be serious.* "Because Jude agreed to this venture?" he snapped. "I really doubt he would." He and Jude hadn't talked in forever and their split hadn't been amicable. Jude had vowed to ignore him, even if he was the last man on earth.

"No, but he'll want to do it," Bob said. "I know him."

"Why? What do you know?" History hadn't been kind to Blake, and there would have to be some serious cash involved to get Jude to sign on.

"I know the song is exploding. It's everywhere and everyone wants to see you together. You two have chemistry. When you sing that song, people believe you love each other," Bob said. "I knew from the moment I heard it you were meant for each other."

At the time, he and Jude had been in love. "Jude won't do it."

"You don't know that."

"I'm pretty sure he won't." The words "*I never want to see you again*" were damn obvious.

"Will you do a tour? Ten to fifteen dates spread over three months? If I set it up?" Bob asked. "If I can get him to go on tour, will you go?"

"Only if he agrees, but I doubt it." Blake shook his head. "You'll have to do some serious magic to get it to work."

"You'll do it?"

"I want out of this fucking movie. I'm tired of being cooped up on the set because I'm not needed." If he could spend time with Jude, then all the better. Maybe he could get them back together and work out his issues…because he loved Jude.

"Consider yourself on tour."

"I film for two more days doing retakes and close-ups," Blake said. "And there's Kel. He'll be pissed. He thinks I'm going to do more movies."

"Let me handle him."

He didn't know how Bob would make this work, but he trusted his old friend. "Once I'm done here, I'm flying out. Where am I going? You're sending an itinerary? Getting a band together? We'll have to do some rehearsals."

"You'll come here to Cleveland. I've got a suite booked at the Crown Hotel and my own recording studio for rehearsals. Two weeks to iron out the wrinkles and you're off," Bob said. "I haven't steered you wrong, have I?"

"No." He'd been a fool to dump Bob as his management, but he'd thought Kel would get him into bigger venues. He'd been wrong. Kel had got him more notice and made him a bona fide star, but it had been a hollow victory. Blake had had to sell out to get to the top.

"This will be good for you. We'll work up a theme. How about a sand, sun and fun theme? Tour dates are firming up as we speak. You'll do three shows a weekend and it'll be great," Bob said. "The career will be back on track and you'll be happy."

"You can do all of that in one summer?"

"If you trust me."

"I trust you." He lived for the thrill of being on the road, holding court on stage and the camaraderie of the touring company. He needed to log miles and play music, but more than that, he needed to talk to Jude. He missed being held, being loved and protected... Jude gave him a place to explore and understood who he was without being judged.

He wanted Jude's kiss, his arms around him and his love. Just because the song was old didn't mean the passion had to have ended. His summer song with Jude had another verse yet to be written.

PUBLISHING

Sign up for our newsletter and find out about all our romance book releases, eBook sales and promotions, sneak peeks and FREE romance books!

About the Author

Megan Slayer, aka Wendi Zwaduk, is a multi-published, award-winning author of more than one-hundred short stories and novels. She's been writing since 2008 and published since 2009. Her stories range from the contemporary and paranormal to LGBTQ and BDSM themes. No matter what the length, her works are always hot, but with a lot of heart. She enjoys giving her characters a second chance at love, no matter what the form. She's been the runner up in the Kink Category at Love Romances Café as well as nominated at the LRC for best author, best contemporary, best ménage and best anthology. Her books have made it to the bestseller lists on Amazon.com.

When she's not writing, Megan spends time with her husband and son as well as three dogs and three cats. She enjoys art, music and racing, but football is her sport of choice.

Megan loves to hear from readers. You can find her contact information, website details and author profile page at https://www.pride-publishing.com